Deliciously

MATED

Ouachita Mountain Shifters, Book 1

P. JAMESON

DELICIOUSLY MATED

Copyright © 2016, P. Jameson
First Electronic Publication: October 2015
All rights reserved.
ISBN: 1537732579
ISBN-13: 978-1537732572

P. Jameson
www.pjamesonbooks.com

Published in the United States of America

First Digital Publication: October 2015
First Print Publication: September 2016

Editing: Tammy Farrell
Formatting and Cover Design: Jatee Photography & Design

DEDICATION

For all the people who are lost, and somehow
find their way even if it takes them off the beaten
path.

ACKNOWLEDGEMENTS

These books wouldn't have been possible without the help of Team PJ. You might be silent, but you are powerful behind the scenes. You know who you are, and I could never thank you enough for standing by my side, lending a shoulder to cry on, and schooling me on where to put commas. To my mister and my little pack-monsters: you are my greatest inspiration. Thank you for supporting me and making sure I'm fed and watered. And for bringing me homemade little gifts to make me smile during deadline (looking at you Big Boo). I love you, my family. To my alpha friend: you have been there since the beginning, holding me up, pushing me forward, cheering me on. Putting up with my crazy days, my insecurities, and my horrible auto-corrected messages. I don't think I've ever been able to express what that means to me. Especially the last part. Just kidding. I love you, my friend.

And finally, to my readers, you amazingly magical motherfluffers: you have pulled me up out of the gutter more times than you know. Your sweet messages and reviews. The personal stories you've shared with me. All of your support just blows me away. Each and every one of you have taken part in this ride with me, and we still have so many miles left! You have found my books and loved them and pushed them to the top, and it means more to me than I even have words for. You are the stars in my eyes. You are the rubber on my tires. You are extraordinary.

ONE

Eagan Masters crossed his arms, rolled his head back on his shoulders, and said a prayer for patience all while managing not to roll his eyes.

Gold star for Eagan! Why don't we get gold stars around this joint anyway?

He stared at the high ceiling of the kitchen, tracing one of the fan ducts across the room with his eyes. It was dusty up there. He should have their handyman, Renner, get someone in to clean it. If there was one thing Eagan didn't tolerate, it was a dirty kitchen.

"Are you fucking listening to me or what? You

need me to yell louder?"

Eagan's head came up to stare blandly at the panther shifter ranting beside him. "No. No, I definitely don't need that."

So Magic was mad. That was clear. The leader of the Ouachita clan of big cats was no gentle creature. As a general rule, he remained pissed at all times, and over the past couple years, he'd actually become pissy-er. Eagan had a feeling it was due to losing two of their people to matings.

Well, *losing* wasn't the right word for it. Technically one of their females, Tana, had only changed clans. She'd joined the Dirt Track Dogs pack after mating one of their wolf shifters. She was still alive and kicking though. That was more than they could say for most female cats that mated. They were either alive or kicking. Never both. And miserable to boot since a mated female often ended up as little more than a baby factory.

It was fact. Mating destroyed females.

It was no good for the males either. Their animals were always left floundering, unable to settle. Unable to have the true bond they wanted.

But Renner, who was in charge of the lodge's construction and day-to-day repairs, he'd mated and he was still around. No loss there.

Still. Magic didn't like it. He tolerated Renner and his human mate, Bethany, because… because…

Well, who the hell knew why. Maybe just because they were so in love you could hardly worry about Renner straying like other male cats did. His panther seemed fully committed which was something Eagan had never seen before. Nevertheless, Magic had made it clear to the clan that no more mating was to take place.

It was mate or clan. You couldn't have both.

Eagan had agreed to the pact because he desperately didn't want to end up like so many males of their kind. He didn't want to be a cheating asshole. He didn't want to betray his mate, whoever she was.

Sure, many of them considered it their right. Mate was important. The *most* important. If she had needs, it was the male's duty to fulfill them, to keep her safe and protected, along with any young he gave her. And in return, he was free to bed as many as he wanted. As many as his cat demanded. The fool animal was the part of them that couldn't commit.

It was the way their animals lived in the wild. Big cat females didn't have permanent mates, but their males provided for them and perpetuated the race. As shifters, their animals struggled with the idea of monogamy, and the human in them lived with the fall-out from that behavior.

Many of Eagan's generation saw the pain this way of living caused, and wanted something different for their future. But Magic was living proof that wanting things to be different doesn't necessarily override a werecat's given instinct to prowl. And because of his past and what happened when he'd tried to mate, he watched Bethany even more closely than Renner did. If she ever showed any hint of distress, he'd skin Renner and hang him by his toes from the nearest tree.

But today, Magic wasn't just pissy. He was angry.

"Tell me what's been taken from the kitchen," he barked, hands gripping the edge of the prep counter as if he were depending on the stainless steel to keep him from murdering Eagan.

"I already told you—"

"Tell me again."

Eagan ground his jaws together. His jaguar didn't like this. He wasn't a beta. Or a submissive of any kind, but sometimes his clan seemed to mistake his kitchen duties as a symbol of weakness.

Fuck that.

Hadn't they ever heard of Gordon *fucking* Ramsay?

Eagan liked to cook and he was good at it. Sometimes they needed their little sexist asses whooped, that's all. Designing meals for his clan took a lot of hard work, and he wouldn't let any of them get away with talking him down.

Not even Magic.

"A sack of potatoes, damn it," he snapped. "There were five. Now four. Add it to your fucking list and quit bitching at me."

Magic's nostrils flared as he pursed his lips.

Eagan gauged him. Maybe they were going to throw down. A regular 'ol cat fight in the kitchen? Hell, he hadn't been in a physical fight in months. No, make that years. And yeah, he needed to blow off steam in a major way.

He sure wasn't blowing it off in the bedroom.

Other cats in their clan satisfied their physical needs by finding temporary lovers in the guests that frequented the lodge. One night stands only. No mating. It was clan law. It was Magic's law.

Unless you were Renner.

But Eagan had had enough one night stands to last him a lifetime. He wanted more. If he couldn't have it, then yeah, bring on a fight.

"A sack of potatoes. That's all you're missing?" Magic growled.

"For fuck's sake, yes."

Magic blew out a furious breath, dragging a

hand through his longish dark locks.

"And this is the first time you've noticed something gone?"

Eagan thought about it. It wasn't *exactly* the first time. It was just the first time such a large item was taken. Little things went missing all the time. A block of cheese. Some caramels from the pantry. Cans of Pringles he hid on a shelf in the back. But he'd always assumed it was his clanmates.

Until today, when Magic went on his inventory rampage.

"Yes," Eagan lied. "This is the first time."

Magic narrowed his eyes. "You're a horrible fucking liar."

Eagan laughed like he always did when he was caught. "And you're a horrible fucking interrogator. What's your problem anyway?"

Magic let out a heavy sigh, tipping his head back. "My problem..." he muttered, running his tongue along his front teeth.

His problem was he needed to get laid. But at

least he'd stopped yelling.

"My problem is we have a *thief*."

Eagan frowned. "What are you talking about? It's just some food. Everyone here works hard—"

"I'm not talking about our cats. It's something else. *Someone* else. If it was a cat, we'd have had a problem years ago."

Eagan shook his head, not following. "Your shit's all messed up over some missing food?"

"No. It isn't just food. It's batteries, flashlights, firewood, rope. Even guests are reporting an alarming amount of missing clothing and toiletries. Mrs. Clemweather's goddamn house slippers went missing from her room last night. And let me tell you, she is *pissed*. Said they cost her ninety dollars at Neiman Marcus or some shit."

"Who the hell buys ninety dollar slippers?"

"Hell if I know. You'd think she'd just grab those fuzzy fuckers from Target or something."

"You'd think," Eagan agreed.

"All I know is, if we don't put a stop to this, it'll ruin our reputation. If people can't feel safe with us in the mountains, our business is fucked. Our clan is fucked."

Eagan nodded. Magic wasn't wrong. Lake Haven had a reputation as a safe place to bring your family to relax and unwind. The last thing they needed was a thief to turn up just before the busy holiday season started.

"Have Gash beef up the security," Eagan suggested.

"He's already on it. He's putting cameras in the guest halls, and turning on the ones outside. Adding one to the back trail too."

"Yeah. Good. But..." Something just didn't make sense. "If it isn't a guest. And it isn't one of us. Who the hell's doing this?"

Magic's jaw ticked. He leaned in, his voice quiet. "Ask yourself this: if they're sly enough to get past us this long, with our ability to scent, and Layna's strict guest records... is there any way in hell they don't know what we are?"

Eagan's mouth went dry. Nobody knew werecats ran the lodge. If they were ever discovered, life as they knew it would be over.

"We have to catch this thief," he breathed.

"Yes," Magic agreed. "And fast."

TWO

One by one, Clara removed the boulders from her loot spot, setting them carefully on the dirt beside her. It was good exercise for her arms. She needed to stay strong. Winter was coming soon and she'd have to prepare her body to survive it.

Preparation was key to hermit life.

Squirrels knew what was up, packing away nuts and seeds for the long cold months. She'd learned so much from watching the animals. The bears had it best though, sleeping away the entire season before waking to the lush spring.

If only she were a bear.

She'd been through five winters. This would be her sixth. Hard to believe she hadn't slept in a real bed, in a home, under a solid roof, for six years.

She paused her digging, letting her reality sink in for a tiny moment. On her own, no family, no friends. No home.

No regrets.

Her lips curved into a smile, and she slowly reached into the crevice between two boulders.

"I see you," she murmured. "One, two, three, four, five... yep, there you are."

Her fingers lingered until the small black lizard with five yellow stripes on his back rested his front feet on her.

Clara clicked her tongue lightly, and the lizard slinked forward.

"I wondered where you'd gone, you flighty little reptile."

There'd been a couple chilly nights already and she'd wondered if her skink had tucked away for the winter. October. She'd seen the calendar during her last loot run. The days were still warm, but the nights brought cool weather. Not cold, but still a stark difference from the hundred degree days she'd grown used to over the summer. If only she had a way to soak up the warmth of the season and store it for winter like she did her other supplies.

The skink quickly slithered up her bare arm and settled on her shoulder, clinging to her tank top strap while Clara went back to digging up the plastic crate she kept her stash in.

When all the rocks were removed, she unlatched the lid and took stock of her supplies. She needed to grab some more socks. And maybe a few more canned goods before it got too cold. But for now, she was going to eat like it was going out of style.

She pulled out five potatoes from the ten pound bag she'd taken from her new gold mine and secured the rest in the plastic bin. Then she collected the butter she'd snuck from the walk-in fridge, a bag of caramels, sour cream and onion

Pringles—yum!—and the bars of chocolate. She left her new slippers in the bin. She'd need them soon, but for now they'd keep with her stash.

One more thing.

Digging to the very bottom of the bin, she found a new bar of soap. Clara held it in her palm, debating. This kind was her favorite. It smelled like lavender. And boy would that be helpful right about now. But... she had to think of the future.

If she planned to continue her raids on the lodge, she needed to be a ghost. She couldn't leave any evidence. Including a scent trail. Because...

There were cat-men running the place. Men who... turned into cats. Not house cats, but big, ferocious, need a lion-tamer cats.

It seemed crazy. It really did. And some days she wondered if her imagination had gone wild, like a shirtless girl on spring break. Maybe six years taking in the wonders of the woods had broken her mind. Whether that was true or not, she'd seen him. A tall, muscled man with bronze hair and pale eyes, stomping through the woods.

He'd given a quick glance around to make sure he wasn't seen, but she was a stealthy observer. Then he'd just... morphed into a massive spotted cat and bounded off in the direction of the river.

And if there was one cat-man, there were more. So, she couldn't take the chance of them smelling her.

She shook her head, tossing the lavender bar back, and dug deeper for the unscented bar she'd grabbed from the hunters last year, stuffing it into her ragged, threadbare backpack. Carefully, she replaced the rocks that concealed her supply crate and stood.

"You ready, skink?" she asked. "I need a bath like you need another tail."

He'd lost his recently. Some danger had threatened, and being the amazing creature he was, he gave them the tail—the lizard version of the middle finger, except... he literally gave them the tail. But it'd grow back with time.

She stared at the lizard on her shoulder, but it didn't talk back. This was a good sign. Perhaps she wasn't losing her mind after all.

The ten minute trek to the small hot springs she used to bathe wasn't too hard. She stayed away from the trails, moving through the trees instead, until she was deep into the woods. People ventured this way occasionally, but it was rare. And when they did, it was usually love-stricken couples looking for a remote romantic location. They ignored her and found somewhere else to makeout. Sometimes they reminded her what her life used to be like. What it felt like to touch and be touched. It had been too many years since she'd felt another person's hands, lips. It would feel foreign and weird now to be kissed now, wouldn't it?

She turned east, closing in on her destination.

She'd chosen this land as hers because of the no hunting laws. She was aware it was private property, and that she was trespassing. But if they couldn't find her, they couldn't kick her out. And she was very, very good at hiding.

But it wasn't until spring that she'd

discovered the lodge tucked away in the mountains near the lake. The no hunting made sense now. With the business nearby, it would be dangerous for hunters to be roaming these woods.

Still. It didn't keep the guns away entirely. There was the occasional poacher from time to time. That was how she'd come into possession of one of the most disgusting things she'd ever had to utilize in her years in the woods. And that was saying something, considering she'd run out of toilet paper several times.

Doe urine. Hunters used it to attract bucks. She'd used it to mask her scent when she needed to go near the lodge.

Clara approached the steaming springs, scanning her surroundings to make sure there wasn't anyone around. She closed her eyes and listened closely, tuning her ears to the sounds of the forest. There was nothing out of the ordinary. She breathed in the moist mountain air, holding it a few seconds before pushing it back out.

She was alone. Just as she wanted to be.

She opened her eyes, slipping the backpack from her shoulder, and her skink from the other one. She set them both on a nearby rock. Skink scurried into a golden sunray and his eyes closed.

Digging through her supplies, she found the soap and began stripping off her clothes. She'd wash the deer scent off her body first, then from her clothes. She brought the items to her nose, testing.

The pungent odor hit her like a punch. She jerked her head back and coughed, gagging.

Or maybe she'd just throw them away.

But no, she needed the jeans. Pants that fit her short legs were hard to find, and she'd need them desperately come winter.

She took the clothes and soap with her to the water and slowly waded in. The heat felt good on her sore muscles. She needed more vitamin B. More greens. She ate the edible ones in the forest, but she'd look at the lodge next time. They probably had fresh spinach.

After setting the smelly clothes on the ground next to the springs, Clara dunked her head beneath the surface of the gurgling water, wetting her thick hair. The harsh, unscented soap was bad for her coarse Latina strands, but she was desperate to get the deer attractant off of her. She smelled like hundred-year-old piss. She'd take the frizzy hair over that any day of the week.

She worked up a lather and spread it through her hair, massaging it all the way down to her scalp. Then she made sure to cover every inch of her body with it.

"Take that, old piss," she muttered, rinsing with the warm water.

She leaned back against the rock, lifting one leg in the air to examine it. Damn. She'd forgotten to look for a razor at the lodge. Finding one that hadn't been used already was going to be tricky, but her old one couldn't cut a peach's fuzz. And besides, she was up for the challenge. The hardest to find items gave her the most satisfaction. It was like a weird game of scavenger hunt. More points for the impossible finds.

She'd give it a few days though, because the thought of donning doe urine again so soon made her want to hurl.

Using the soap and a rock, she scrubbed her clothes clean, giving up on the tank top. Then she wrung them out and set them in the sun to dry. Resting on the rock next to her skink, she let the remaining rays of sun lap up the water from her body.

Closing her eyes, she felt herself relax in the woods that had become a home for her. The woods that had taken her in and comforted her after she'd been tossed into an unavoidable tragedy.

No. Don't think about it.

The screech of a bird in the sky above had her jerking her eyes open. It was too close to the sound of a baby crying. A flock of them followed, reminding her of her own crying, and the crying of others. There had been so many tears. So many aching wails. So much pain.

The sun reflecting off the surface of the water did nothing to warm her. It sent a chill down her spine. It looked like twisted metal. The drip, drip, drip of the water falling from her hair onto the rock below reminded her of—

No. There was no remembering the past in her woods. There was only moving forward. Surviving. And finding peace in her situation. There was only the basics. Never again would she allow material things to distract her from the important parts of life.

Reaching into her bag, she pulled out her two ratted notebooks. They were identical on the outside, but inside, they contained very different writings. She opened the one that had a pen sticking out of the spiral, and flipped to a blank page.

Today was a good day. Cool nights have arrived, but I don't dread the coming winter as much as I usually might. I'll miss Skink and the animals of course, but still, after living in the woods for all this time, I've never been more sure that this is what my life should be. I have no desire to reinsert myself back into humanity. I'm a woman in love. With the solitude. With the loneliness. I'm as happy as I deserve to be. It was a good day.

Clara closed the notebook. Record keeping was also important for hermitting. With no one around to witness her life but herself, it was crucial to write everything down. Not because anyone would come along and read it, but for herself. Countless times, she'd read back through her journals and found memories she'd already forgotten. In some strange way, it kept her feeling... real. It reminded her she existed even though she'd done her best to appear like she didn't.

Being a ghost was hard.

Clara laid back on the rock, sighing. She'd rest for just a while. Then she'd head back to her camp and cook up those potatoes. She needed to carb load. Feed that layer of fat that would keep her alive through the cold months. And with the discovery of the lodge, this was going to be her easiest winter yet.

Clara smiled. Life was good.

THREE

The knife sliced through the onion in short, quick intervals that banged out a staccato rhythm against the cutting board. Eagan was in the zone as he whirled through the prep work for tomorrow's meals. Normally he'd leave this job to Bailey, his assistant. But he'd been sticking around the kitchen more the past few days, keeping his eyes open for any clue that would reveal the thief.

Gash, the clan's security guy, had beefed up the monitoring, but there'd been nothing out of the ordinary lately. No guests missing items that weren't in the lost and found. No food had been pilfered. No people who weren't on the guest register or employees.

But the thief would be back. And then the hunt would be on.

All the cats had been alerted. There would be plenty of shifter noses sniffing around for the bastard.

Eagan moved on to the carrots, slicing the entire bunch of them into uniform medallions.

He wondered how Magic would handle the thief when they caught him. Magic didn't like dealing with the police. More likely, he'd scare the human half to death and send him on his way.

Layna burst through the swinging kitchen door with an annoyed look on her face. Renner's sister was oddly like the female version of Magic. She took no shit, but she gave a lot of it. Eagan guessed it was why the two of them managed the lodge so well. He was the muscle behind the operation, and she was the brains, keeping records and schedules and making sure the guests were happy at all times.

She held the cordless phone out to him. "Destiny's calling," she said wryly. Then one side of her mouth lifted. "I've been wanting to say that *forever*."

Eagan frowned, wiping his hands on a nearby towel. "Destiny? Prego by an asshole wolf Destiny?"

Destiny was a bobcat shifter and member of the Dirt Tracks Dogs, the same hybrid pack that Tana belonged to. She'd stayed at the lodge for a short time after she'd become pregnant by one of the wolves. Eagan had—and he'd never admit this out loud—really enjoyed keeping her well-fed and cared for. There was something special about making sure a female had the necessary nutrients and energy to grow young.

Layna rolled her eyes. "Do you know another one? Besides yours I mean. Your withered future? Your fate. Your—"

"Give me that, you smartass." He snatched the phone from her grasp and she let out a laugh that reminded him of a cartoon villain as she walked off.

Eagan pressed the receiver to his ear. "Hello."

"Hey, Eagan, this is Destiny." She hesitated as if gauging his memory of her.

"Knocked up pasta lover. Yeah, I remember you," he said, sarcastically.

"Ha. Ha. Ha. I wasn't sure if I'd made a mark."

Destiny ended up mating the wolf shifter who fathered her young, and had recently become their Elder, a foreseer for her pack. It was a concept Eagan didn't necessarily understand. The cats didn't have wise people to guide them. And even though she was a werecat herself, she'd been chosen and trained to be a guide for her wolf pack.

"Barely," he said.

"Hmm. I remember you being a tad nicer when I was visiting the lodge. Maybe I'm talking to the wrong Eagan. Is there another one around?"

"Nope. Just me." He chuckled. "What can I do for you, Destiny? You got a prego craving? Need the recipe for that chicken marsala?"

Pregnant. Damn, what he wouldn't give to have a female of his own to start a family with. Sometimes at night, he let himself dream about it. A female to love, belly swollen with a baby he'd put there. No midnight craving would go unanswered. Lasagna at 2am? No problem. He'd knock that shit out before she could blink twice. Then he'd feed her. She wouldn't even have to pick up a fork. He'd love the fuck out of his female, and she'd know it.

Eagan's thoughts turned dark.

The cats weren't meant to love. Only to procreate. They weren't monogamous. He'd only hurt any female he chose. He'd seen his father do it. His grandfather even. If Magic hadn't shown him a different way, a mating abstinence, maybe he'd have done it too, sleeping with as many females as his feral jag desired while his female grew their cubs and warmed their home.

But when he lay in his bed alone at night, he didn't feel like that kind of man. He felt like he could be happy loving only one female for his entire life, making her his queen, satisfying her every need. Like those goddamn wolves from DTD. Like… Renner.

"Actually, now that you mention it," Destiny mused over the line, her voice turning dreamy, "I *would* like that recipe. I've been *dying* for just a taste…"

"You got it. I'll have Layna email it to you."

"But that's not the reason I called."

"Oh?"

"Yeah, no. Um… I have a… well, I had a vision…"

Eagan braced his hip against the counter. "A vision."

"Mm hm. A perk of the job."

"Oh. Like a Theresa Caputo thing?"

"What? That woman from TV, the Long Island medium? No. It's nothing like that." She paused. "Well, maybe it's a little like that. Look, I just wanted to tell you something that might come in handy soon. God, maybe this was a mistake," she muttered.

"Wait. Your vision was about *me*?"

"Duh. You think I'd just dial you up to chat about my freaky psychic crap? Listen, you make a mean marsala, but we ain't tight like that."

"Agreed." He tucked the phone against his shoulder and moved into the dining room to sit on one of the polished wood benches. "So tell me about this vision."

"Well… I can't. It doesn't work like that."

Eagan rolled his eyes. "Good god, woman. Will you tell me what you need to tell me?"

There was a harsh, low growl from the other end of the line, and then Destiny's muffled voice. "It's okay, Diz." Her wolf mate must have heard him through the phone. "He's just anxious."

Eagan frowned. *Was* he anxious? The way he was gripping the phone made it seem like he was. Yeah, okay. He wanted to know what Destiny had seen and how it related to him.

"Listen, okay," she rushed out. "When you find the book that doesn't belong to you… read it."

"Wait, what. That's it? That's the message you have for me?"

A sigh came across the line. "I'm new at this, okay? It's the best I've got. Just... do what I said. *Read it.*"

Eagan shook his head, completely baffled by the conversation. "Yeah, alright."

"And send that recipe."

"Got it."

"And get some sleep."

"What?"

"Meh. I figure everyone could use a little extra sleep."

Eagan closed his eyes, exasperated. "Goodbye, Destiny."

"See ya."

He hung up, and set the phone on the table, leaning forward on his elbows.

What the hell kind of foreseer was Destiny anyways? Clearly she wasn't any good at this Elder thing yet. Maybe they ripened with time.

Eagan stared out the picture window. It was

dark outside, nearing 10 pm. The only light was from the string of electric lanterns around the perimeter of the lodge. Guests and employees alike had taken to their rooms for the night.

He should get home himself, do what she said and get some sleep. But too much time in the cabin only reminded him how alone he was. How much he was missing.

"You got a good thing going here," Eagan murmured under his breath. And it was true. He *did* have it good here. They all did. But that didn't keep him from wanting more. Forsaking his nature to mate was the price to pay for being loyal to his clan.

Sometimes he thought it was worth it.

Sometimes he knew it was.

He spun the phone on the table top, watching as it slowed to a stop before repeating the process.

A clatter from the kitchen had him jerking to attention.

"Damn it, Layna. Don't touch my shit. I'll put

the phone up. Go to bed."

There was no answer.

"Layna?"

Eagan stood from the bench and crept toward the back entrance to the kitchen. He eased the door open, but saw nothing out of the ordinary. Stepping in, he scanned the prep area, quickly finding the source of the noise. His heavy chef's knife lay on the tile floor.

Eagan let out an exhausted sigh. He must've set it too close to the edge, causing it to fall.

He strolled over to his work station and began packaging the chopped veggies for the walk-in. As he worked, his nose burned with the smell that filled the room.

"Damn onions," he muttered to himself.

Walking to the freezer with his stack of containers, he nearly tripped over his knife. He bent to pick it up and tossed it in the wash sink before reaching for the handle of the walk-in. But what he saw there locked his muscles in place.

There was a smudge of dirt on the chrome of

the handle. Not dust. Dirt. Dark, like the mud from the creek bottom. He was sure it hadn't been there earlier.

The back of his neck prickled with the sense of danger. Their thief was here, and Eagan's cat wanted out to fight. To defend. Catch his prey.

Not here. Not inside. No turning in the lodge.

But before he could come up with a plan, the door to the storage closet burst open and a small, dark figure shoved past him, sending the containers of onions to the floor.

"Shit!"

Eagan spun, reaching for the figure, and managed to grasp one mud-covered arm. A jolt of recognition hit him, and his throat tightened, his jaguar reeling at the contact.

He jerked angrily, and the intruder gasped, turning to gawk at him from under the bill of a ratted baseball cap.

His breath froze in his chest.

Golden eyes fringed in long dark lashes stared back at him. Muddied round cheeks sat above the most luscious set of rosebud lips he'd ever seen. Lips that were parted in shock. And probably pain. Pain?

Fuck.

Their thief was a female.

He loosened his grip, but that was a huge mistake. Because the moment he did, she jerked away from him hard enough that he stumbled backward. And before he'd even regained his footing, she ran.

"Wait!"

Eagan scrambled to catch her, but she was through the swinging door before he could. He pushed through, looking left and then right. Both ways again, and there was no sign of her. But she must've made a run for the outdoors. She wouldn't stay inside where she could be captured.

He rushed through the lobby and out the front, stopping on the front deck to scan the area. No sign of his thief.

"Shit."

He breathed deep, trying to find her scent.

But he only smelled the normal scents of the lodge. The werecats, the human, the forest. The deer.

He ran into the clearing where cars were parked, ducking and searching under each one. But there was no thief.

He walked the perimeter of the main building, sniffing for any change that could indicate the female, and came up with nothing.

Eagan stared out into the forest. He could track her if only he had a scent. Without it, in the dark… he had nothing to go on. She was a ghost.

"Shit."

His eyes caught on one of the new cameras Gash had installed, and a smile crept up his lips. He'd go now, and find her with the cameras. What were the chances she'd escaped them all?

Running for the front door, he bounded into the lobby and stopped short.

There, on the polished wood floor, was an old notebook with a pen sticking out of the spine. Eagan bent to examine it. It was small, about the size of a 5x7 picture, and the edges of the cover were worn dirty and curling from use.

It wasn't there when he'd run through minutes ago.

He picked it up, bringing it to his nose and breathing in deep. Ah, yes. A smile curved his lips. This belonged to her. And damn, was his thief smart.

He shook his head in disbelief.

Not only had she anticipated he'd run outside first, she'd found an ingenious way to mask her scent so she couldn't be tracked. Doe urine.

He stared at the notebook, turning it in his fingers. His only clue. This, however, was an accident. *This* would get her caught.

Eagan stood, and when he did, Destiny's words came back to him.

Fucking hell.

When you find the book that isn't yours... read it.

Oh, he'd read it alright. He was going to find his thief before she could do anymore damage.

FOUR

She shouldn't have gone near the onions. But they were the red kind, and it'd been so long since she'd smelled fresh chopped onions. Who knew she'd miss *that*?

Damn it.

She was caught, and by a familiar face. Her man from the woods. The one she'd seen turn into a spotted cat. He was the one who found her in the kitchen. Same rusty blond hair, same deep gray eyes, but he was even better up close. She'd been only inches away from his full lips and that angled jaw. Once upon a time those characteristics would have set her heart to pumping.

Now her heart pounded for an entirely different reason.

Clara rubbed her arm where his giant hand had grabbed her. It didn't hurt. It tingled. The first time she'd been touched in six years. It made her throat close up with too many emotions. And even though she shouldn't, even though it was dangerous... it made her want for more.

She shook the thought away.

Now she was stuck here indoors. *Inside* the lodge. Where she could be caught. And this time, if she was arrested she'd actually be charged for the crime.

Dread slammed her hard. She squeezed her eyes closed in fear.

Stealing. That's what she'd really been doing all this time. Taking what wasn't hers in order to survive. Because she couldn't bear the thought of being part of the real world.

She was a thief. And no matter how much she liked to think of herself as Robin Hood, she wasn't.

Her only saving grace was that she intended on paying it back. Someday. When she was ready to emerge from the woods and face reality. *If* she was ever ready. She kept meticulous records. Every last thing she'd ever taken was written down.

She pushed her guilt to the back of her mind. Right now she had to focus on getting out of this place. She'd noticed the tightened security. Noticed the new cameras. They'd prevented her from going to the guest rooms. And she'd had to find a new way into the lodge. Which hadn't been hard. She wondered if they knew their alarm system was down.

Whatever. She wasn't going to be the one to tell them.

Slipping past the lobby was easy. There was only one camera in the far corner by the door. From there, she found another short hallway that seemed to be clear of any recording devices. She avoided the door marked OFFICE and kept going. If she could find an open room with a window…

on this side of the building, she could just climb out and slip into the trees.

She tried the next door, and it was locked. One that looked like a storage closet, and it was locked too. Finally, she came to a set of double doors. The frosted glass and etched lettering that read SPA seemed too modern for the wood-on-wood country feel of the lodge. Testing the handle, it opened.

She frowned, surprised. Why was this door the only unlocked one in the hall?

Clara stepped back. What if someone was in there? What if she was trapping herself inside? What if—

The sound of a door slamming and footsteps made the decision for her. She cranked the handle and stepped into the room, hoping against hope that she'd find herself alone in the spa.

It was dark inside, the light of the moon filtering in through the wood framed glass walls. She was quiet for several seconds, listening for any sign that someone was around, but it appeared she was alone.

Laughter from outside the spa had her scrambling for a hiding spot. She ducked under a counter just as the door swung open.

"Renner! Just give me a second, okay? I forgot to lock up," a female voice managed through a round of giggles.

"I don't want to give you a second, Bethy." The response was male and husky with desire.

Clara rolled her eyes. Damn it all. If she got stuck in here waiting for some stupid couple to finish making out, she was going to barf.

"Layna's watching Rhys and every time I see you standing here in this place..." An odd sound erupted from his throat. Like a cat purring, but rougher. The soft sounds of kissing drifted to Clara's ears. "This is where it all started," he whispered. "Where we found each other again after all those years. I fucking love seeing you in here. I want you now. Like this. Against the counter."

God, no. Please, no.

The woman moaned and Clara crossed her fingers that they weren't about to get it on with her right there in the room.

"Renner…" The plea was followed by a yelp and more giggling.

Good god. Didn't these lovebirds have a curfew?

A sharp whoosh indicated the door opening.

"Shit," the man cursed. "Damn it, Eagan. Ever think about knocking?"

"On the spa? No. It never occurred to me."

Clara froze. That voice. It was the man from the kitchen. The one who'd touched her. The one with stormy eyes. They reminded her of the sky before it rained.

"No. I can't say it ever occurred to me."

"Well, maybe it should occur to you *next time*."

"Maybe *next time*, you should get a room." There was a loud hiss and then Eagan laughed. "Just saying."

"What are you doing in here?" the horny

guy—Renner?—asked.

"I heard something. Just thought I'd check." He sounded disturbed, and Clara realized he'd probably thought the noise was her.

"Oh no," the woman murmured concerned. "Was it the thief again? Have more things gone missing?"

Clara's stomach cramped. The thief. They were talking about her.

Eagan with the stormy eyes hesitated. "Nah. No, I'm just keeping my ears open lately. You guys see anything?"

"No," the woman said. "Nothing since the meeting last week. Magic said we should watch out, but everything seems normal around here."

Clara couldn't breathe. He'd lied to his friends about her. Why? Why hadn't he given her up?

"Do you..." the horny guy began, sounding confused. "Do you scent... *doe*?"

Shit. The hunting attractant was useful as long as she was in and out quick. But trapped in a room...

"Oh, uh... yeah," Eagan laughed. "It's this notebook."

Notebook. Clara scrunched her face up. The shit just kept hitting the fan.

Please don't let it be mine.

"It smells like a deer?" the woman asked, skeptically.

"Yeah. Weird, huh?"

The other man grunted. "What is it?"

"Something for the lost and found," Eagan muttered. "You guys locking up or what?"

"Yep," the woman said. "Let's go."

There was some rhythmic electronic beeping and then the door clicked shut and Clara could hear their fading conversation down the hall. She counted to ten, just to be sure they were gone, and then rushed to shrug her bag from her shoulders.

Please, oh please...

But right away her fears were confirmed. The thin material of her backpack was gaping on the bottom right corner. She'd caught it on something. Or maybe it ripped when the cook grabbed her.

"Damn it," she breathed and then smacked her palm over her mouth. No talking. Not even a whisper. She didn't know if the cat-man had super hearing, but she couldn't chance it. And with the purring and talk of scenting... maybe they were all cat-men. And women. Maybe she'd stumbled onto a different realm. Like The Labyrinth or something.

Stop it. Stop thinking crazy. You aren't crazy. Being alone doesn't make you crazy.

Clara nodded to herself. She wasn't crazy. She knew what she saw.

Digging in her backpack, she found one of her notebooks. But sure enough, the other was missing. A sinking feeling settled in the pit of her stomach, and her hands shook as she peeled back the cover to see which one she'd lost.

Today was a good day...

No. No, no, no.

Tears pricked her eyes, threatening to overspill and run down her muddy cheeks.

This was her journal. This was the least

important of the two books. The journal made her feel alive. Reminded her she existed. But the other one? She *needed* that other book. Without it... without it she couldn't live with herself. And worse, if someone found that book, they'd have all the evidence they needed to lock her up for a long time.

Shaking, she tried to think. There had to be a way to get it back.

The lost and found. The cook said he was putting it in the lost and found. Maybe she could retrieve it.

Clara looked around. It was her habit to make use of the things around her. To utilize every available asset at her disposal. The spa afforded her an opportunity to get clean. Could she use that it to get her book back? Maybe clean up enough to look like a guest? Could she walk up to the front desk and ask for the lost and found? Without freezing up. Without appearing like a bedraggled forest urchin.

She hadn't spoken to another human in six

years. Only her skink and the other animals. And herself.

God.

But she had to try. She had to get that book. It was crucial.

Okay.

Okay, she was doing this.

Clara nodded, closing her backpack and tying the strap around the end so she wouldn't lose anything else. She crawled from under the counter and made her way carefully to the back of the spa where the showers were. The dim track lighting offered her enough glow to get a picture of her surroundings.

A small row of lockers painted a soothing blue stood outside the door. She tested one and it opened. Inside was a blue sweater and a pair of white slacks. The pants wouldn't fit her, but the shirt might work.

The wall behind her was lined with shelves full of product. Clara scanned the array of shampoos, body washes, and lotions. Her eyes landed on an herbal hair removal remedy. She squinted as she read the instructions on the back. She was skeptical that it could work on her coarse, dark leg hair, but she was desperate. Her search for a razor had resulted in nil.

She tucked it into her elbow and grabbed some shampoo, conditioner, and soap from the shelf before ducking into the shower room.

Clara stopped just inside the door, gawking at the elaborate setup. Three stalls lined one wall, each with mosaic tiled doors framed in smooth river rock. Carefully, she set her things on the nearby bench and took a deep breath. She could do this. It was a shower. How hard could it be?

Stepping forward, she pulled on the handle of the middle stall. It came open with a snap, making her jump at the noise.

She kept still. Listening. But everything was quiet.

Pulling the door all the way open, she examined the inside. Okay, so it was your typical slide-on faucet. No funky computer mojo. She could handle that.

Clara stepped back and caught sight of herself in the mirror that took up the entire wall opposite the shower. What she saw choked her heart in her chest. That couldn't be her. Could it? She'd seen her reflection in dark windows and in the calm of the streams she bathed in, and it hadn't seemed so... frightening. Her outside matched her inside now.

Tainted.

Haunted. She *was* a ghost but not the kind she'd intended to be.

She took a step forward and the reflection moved too.

She was thicker than she'd been a few months ago. She knew because her clothes fit tighter. And it made sense as she was prepping for the winter. But she was much thinner than when she'd last looked at herself in an actual mirror.

She removed the ball cap she'd used to hide her hair. The dull brown stuff that tumbled out looked like burnt straw.

Clara's eyes searched frantically for anything that looked like her. Anything that she could connect with. Something that would make her think, *that's me*. She wasn't the same person she'd been when she walked into the woods, but surely there must be something for her to hold to.

Her face was covered in mud that she'd put there in order to blend more fully into the night. But her lips maybe. Yeah, maybe they were familiar. They'd always been full. Kissable, her sister had called them.

Somehow she found her eyes, her gaze clashing with the mirror's.

There. There she was. In the eyes.

That's me.

The thought was reassuring. It calmed her. No matter what she looked like, no matter how long she'd been away from civilization, she was still her. Clara Destacio.

Reaching up, she fingered her straw hair. It had grown long. Nearly to her waist. Maybe the spa quality product would help tame it.

With a sigh, she stripped off her muddy clothes, shoving the shirt and cap in a nearby trashcan. Once again, she'd have to salvage her jeans. Her boots and socks, she tucked in a corner by the bench.

Reaching into the shower, she turned on the water to let it get warm. When it came to temperature, she gingerly stepped into the stall, bringing the soap with her. But as soon as she did, water began shooting in pulsating streams starting from her head and moving down her body.

A yelp clawed its way up her throat but she stifled it with her hand.

The shower was motion activated.

Clara pressed her hand to her chest, willing her heart to remember its normal rhythm. She needed to hurry in case someone noticed the noise from the shower. She didn't know for sure how insulated this room was. And getting caught with her pants down would be the ultimate embarrassment.

But the water felt so damn good. With the hot springs that were abundant in this area of Arkansas, she had warm water to bathe with. But a shower... water spraying over her body like warm summer rain... that was a privilege she didn't get often.

She let the vacillating streams wash the mud and smelly junk from her body. Staring at the tile beneath her feet, she watched as the water went from mucky brown to clear. Then she went to work on her hair. She washed it twice with the sweet smelling shampoo before coating it in conditioner and letting it rest while she tackled her legs.

Following the instructions, she mixed the herbal powder into a paste and rubbed it over her legs, keeping them out of the stream of water. She was supposed to wait ten minutes but maybe it'd work faster. Ten minutes more under the shower seemed risky.

While she waited, she thought about her situation. Eagan The Cook. He was handsome as the sun was hot. He probably knew it too. She'd known many guys like him in her former life. Had relationships with some. It wasn't anything she missed. Relationships. Not with her family. Not with her friends. And certainly not with any muscle bound hormone-ridden hot heads.

He was the only one who knew what she looked like. For whatever reason, he'd kept her break-in to himself. If she could avoid him, surely she could get her book back. It would be quick-like. One night inside, and then talk to whoever manned the front desk tomorrow. She'd be back at her camp before she knew it.

Clara moved and realized the paste on her legs had transformed into a semi-hard shell.

Whoa. Now what?

The directions said remove the mask carefully but quickly, in swift downward motions. Aw, crap. This was going to hurt like hell.

Shoring up her courage, she grasped a spot just above her knee and jerked down hard.

She let out a gasp as searing pain shot from

her leg to a spot between her eyes, tapping there like a hammer against a nail.

Satan's hot hairy mama. What fresh hell had she gotten herself into?

Sticking her leg directly in the stream of hot water, she attempted to wash away the paste, but it was no dice. The stuff was like cement mixed with cockroach shells—because those things are indestructible.

Clara looked around. She didn't have any more time to waste. She needed to clean up here and find a place to stow away until morning.

Her poor, poor legs. She was going to have to do this the hard way.

Gripping another piece of the shell, she counted to three in her head. But her hands didn't move.

Come onnnn, Destacio. Sucker up.

One, two, three. Pull.

A bigger strip came off this time, and Clara's throat constricted around a cry. Before she could think about it anymore, she yanked another piece, and then another, tears mixing with the warm water of the shower. When one leg was free of hair, she went after the other one, scraping at the mask with her nails until there was nothing of it left.

Panting and raw, she leaned against the tiled wall and watched as the clay collected around the drain.

Holy shit. Holy freaking shit.

She took a deep breath, forcing herself into action.

Rinse hair. Now.

She contorted so the water couldn't hit her tender legs, and scrubbed vigorously at her mop until all the conditioner was gone. Then she turned the water off and burst from the stall. Snatching a towel from the shelf nearby, she wrapped it around her head and went back for another. She leaned against the counter to catch her breath and shot a glare at the open shower door.

The shower from hell. She never wanted to

shower again. Give her a natural hot spring bath any day.

Clara squeezed her eyes closed, breathing deep to calm her nerves.

Just a little longer. Just a little more work to do. Then she'd have her book, and she'd go home. To her skink. To her mattress made of a sleeping bag and newspapers.

Just a little longer.

FIVE

The lunch rush was over and the kitchen was prepping for dinner, their biggest meal of the day. But all Eagan could think about was a dirty little female and her notebook he had stuffed in his back pocket.

He'd skimmed the contents fifty times since finding it in the lobby but it still didn't make any sense. Destiny definitely needed to explain herself. But she hadn't returned his calls. He'd done what she said. Read the book. Now what?

Eagan stirred the giant pot of beef stew before sliding a pan of cheddar biscuits into the oven.

"We need the cobblers in now," he called over his shoulder.

"Almost done with the peach," Bailey replied, short of breath. The tiger was usually quick on her toes, but she was lagging today.

"Blueberry?"

"Done. Counter behind you."

Eagan twisted, grabbing the tray and sliding it into the lower oven.

Layna pushed through the kitchen doors as he was closing the oven. She held the phone up. "Destiny is calling... again." She frowned. "Never thought I'd get to say that twice."

"Finally," Eagan huffed, reaching for the receiver. But Layna held it behind her back out of his reach.

"There's something you should know first—"

Eagan scowled. "Give me the fucking phone."

One eyebrow came up, and she smiled ruefully. "Fine." She passed the phone to him and turned to leave. "It's your damn funeral."

Eagan stepped out from behind the prep counter and pushed the speaker to his ear.

The first thing he heard was a gruesome scream. His blood ran cold at the sound. Something was wrong.

"Destiny?"

"WHAT?!"

Eagan winced, pulling the phone away from his ear.

The hell?

A tortured moan came from the other end of the earpiece, and then, "How much longer? I can't do this three tiiiiimes."

"Give me the phone." Diz's voice came calmly in the wake of Destiny's roar. Her mate was nearby. Good sign. At least she wasn't alone. But was she alright? Were her triplets okay?

"No. I can talk. I need to talk... just..." Another roar of pain cut off her words.

Holy shit.

There were countless minutes of heavy breathing and then she finally sounded normal.

Sort of.

"Eagan? You still there?"

"Uh…" Was the right answer yes? "Yes?"

"Good, okay. Make this quick because another contraction will happen in about… one minute."

Contraction. Oh… damn. Destiny was in labor.

"This about the book?" she asked when Eagan remained silent.

"Yeah. Uh… you sure you want to do this now?"

"I'm sure. What's up?" She said the words as if she hadn't chomped his ear off just seconds ago.

"You said to read it."

"That's right."

"And I did."

"Perfect!" she exclaimed as if the book held some secret to life.

"But it doesn't make any sense."

"What do you mean?"

Eagan turned to face the wall even though that wouldn't keep Bailey from overhearing the conversation.

"All it is, is page after page of lists. Random things and amounts. Foods, brand names, things like that. And dates. And addresses. There's no rhyme to it. It's just an eternity long list."

"Ahh," Destiny said.

"Ah?"

"You read the wrong book."

Eagan frowned. "Wrong book?"

"Or maybe the right one. I can't be sure."

A whimper passed through the line.

"Destiny, that makes no sense." His voice rose with frustration.

"Because you read the *wrong* goddamn *MOTHERFUCKING* BOOK!" And then another agony-induced scream ripped through the phone.

"Okay, okay." Eagan tried for a placating tone. "I'll just, you know, read all the books that I find that aren't mine and hope one of them makes sense."

"Yeah," she snapped. "You do that." And then the line clicked dead.

Eagan looked at the phone, wondering if that

had really just happened. Destiny was a sweet female. She'd never raised her voice even once when she'd stayed at the lodge.

"A small cat having wolf babies," Bailey murmured. "That has to hurt."

Eagan turned to look at her. Bailey had a point. Destiny wasn't like the cats around the lodge. She was a wild species, but definitely not considered large.

"Bethany is human and she had a panther baby. I don't remember her turning murderous."

Bailey laughed, her short brown curls bouncing with her movement. "You weren't there for the delivery. Should've seen Doc Davis. She had nail marks the whole length of her arms."

Eagan's eyes peeled wide. "Doc let a human mark her up?"

Bailey shrugged, pushing the peach cobbler into the oven. "She's all about patient care. Plus, I think she felt sorry for her."

Eagan shook his head. He didn't know the first thing about females having young. Probably would never learn either.

He handed the phone to Bailey. "Take this back to Layna, would you?"

"Sure thing, boss."

Dinner time came, and the dining room filled with guests and employees. Eagan stayed busy, prepping dishes while the waiters served them. But his mind remained where it had been all day. On the thief and the book. The way his heart had hammered when he touched her. The way her muddied face looked as she'd stared up at him, knowing she was caught. She was a mouse to his cat. Or so he'd thought. Until she outsmarted him.

And the book.

Was it a wish list? Things she was looking to steal? Maybe she was contracted to steal the items and made money when she delivered. Except that didn't sit well with him. She wasn't stealing high-priced items from the lodge. The things they were missing were small time. Camping supplies, food, clothing...

Survival supplies he realized.

Eagan's grip tightened on the rag he was using to wipe down the counter.

Survival. Was that why his thief was stealing?

He pulled the notebook from his back pocket and flipped through the pages.

One quart, whole milk

One loaf bread, whole wheat

Processed cheese singles, 24 ct.

He skipped a few pages.

AA batteries

Lighter fluid

Weather radio

Pocket knife, five inch

Lavender soap, one bar

His heart raced. His mouth hung agape as he turned page after page, finding similar items. He skipped back to the beginning to note the dates. The earliest one was nearly six years ago.

Six years.

Eagan swallowed the lump in his throat. Finger leading his eyes, he combed through each page. Fishing rods, tackle, a variety of tools, a hairbrush, toilet paper. The next page had only one item listed.

Box full of scrap paper/cardboard

The words had been scratched out and replaced with,

Box full of love letters

Irreplaceable

Put off burning them as long as I could. Almost too long. I'm so sorry, Rose and Arnold.

Forgive me.

Eagan stood there so long, staring at that page, reading it over and over. When he finally looked up, the kitchen was clean and Bailey was gone.

Irreplaceable.

He thumbed through the book again. These were notes. Records of what she'd taken over the years. There was only one reason she'd keep track. It was because she intended on paying it all back.

His thief… she was homeless. She took the things she needed to survive. And she planned on making amends one day.

Eagan's chest ached.

What had happened to her? Why was she alone in the woods and homeless for so long? When he'd grabbed her, she hadn't said a word, but he could feel her surprise. The way her eyes went wide. When was the last time she'd been touched? The last time she'd interacted with other people?

His mind churned, desperately needing to understand her.

Eagan tucked the notebook back into his pocket and ran a hand through his spiky hair as he paced the tiled floor. She'd be back. She'd need to eat. And he had a feeling she wouldn't leave her book.

He knew what to do.

He was going to set a trap and catch her. Make her answer his questions. Make him understand why his jag was chuffing inside, demanding he keep her visit last night a secret.

Eagan rushed to the walk-in to find the

leftover stew. All the remaining food from the day was open to whoever wanted it. Usually cats who'd missed dinner would come scrounging for it, but it was so late, they were likely done for the night. Piling his arms full of cobbler and biscuits, he brought it all to the counter. Luckily, it was still warm.

Reaching over the counter, he pulled down some to-go containers, filling the first to the brim with the hearty stew he'd made for the lodge. He added a drizzle of sour cream and a sprig of parsley before putting the lid on. The second container, he filled with Bailey's cobblers. One piece of each, in case his female didn't like one of the flavors. He bagged up several biscuits and added them, along with a napkin and utensils to the pile of offerings.

Rubbing his palms together, he stood back, looking at the food. Something was missing.

Ah, yes. He snapped his fingers, and then bent to retrieve a small saucepan. Setting it on the stove, he turned the burner to low and went to the pantry for chocolate. He broke the bar into pieces and added them to the pan, pouring in milk and a dash of vanilla and cinnamon. The early October nights were chilly. She'd appreciate his specialty hot chocolate to keep her warm.

Damn. His stomach cramped at the thought of where she must live. The cats knew these woods like their own names. If she was in a tent or a cabin, they'd know of it. And she was certainly nearby or she wouldn't frequent the lodge for her necessities. He imagined her holing up in a cave or sleeping in the trees like fucking Katniss or something.

A protective instinct rose up in him. He didn't know her or how she came to be such a clever thief, but the need to help her clawed at him inside. He couldn't rat her out to Magic. Not yet. Not until he at least tried to make this better.

Eagan shook his head.

As adept as she was at stealing, she was probably fine. But he had to know for sure. Food was the way.

He stirred the chocolate until it was smooth and steaming, and then he poured it into a foam cup. He added a dollop of whipped cream, another sprinkle of cinnamon, and then the lid.

There. Everything was perfect.

He cleaned up the new mess he'd made, jotted a note for his thief, took one last look at his work, and then forced himself out the door.

She'd come tonight. He knew it. The book was too important.

SIX

Sneaking into the lodge this time seemed harder. Not because they'd added anymore security measures. In fact, Clara was pretty sure the cook hadn't outed her. Leaving this morning had been too easy. Nobody even looked at her twice. She'd managed to find the lost and found without speaking to anybody. She'd guessed it was behind the front counter and rummaged through it early, when the lady who manned it was getting her coffee.

Her book was nowhere to be found. Which meant the cook kept it. Which meant she could return to the lodge and search the kitchen for it, taking a huge risk of getting caught. Or leave her perfect place in the woods to avoid jail. But that meant giving up on the idea of ever paying back all the people she'd wronged. It meant the wrongs she'd inherited, the ones she'd been avoiding while she hermitted away in the forest, would continue to haunt her.

It was unacceptable.

She was willing to risk her freedom this once.

The journal was important to her. It was a chance at redemption, even if just a little. Somehow she'd find a way to get it back without going to jail. She just had to be smart.

Clara swallowed the bile in her throat as she slinked through the empty hall toward the lobby. The entire inside of the main building was decked out in creepy fake cobwebs, sparkly pumpkins, and haunted house cutouts. By the door was a vampire statue with red blinking lights for eyes.

Halloween was coming. The idea brought a smile to her face. It was always one of her favorite holidays. As a child, she'd loved dressing up in her mom's homemade costumes. For a few hours she could be someone else. Not a Destacio. Not a rich kid showered in too many expensive things. Not the daughter of a careless alcoholic father. But a princess or a witch or Minnie Mouse or whatever her imagination wanted. She could be scary if she wanted, and growl at the kids who made fun of her. Or she could ignore them altogether because it was Halloween and it didn't matter what ugly thing they said about her. Sometimes she'd even wished she could actually be what she dressed up as. Someone new altogether.

That desire didn't fade as she grew. And now she *was* someone else. The Clara Destacio she'd been born as was transformed. Like Teen Wolf or something. She almost giggled as an image of the old Michael J. Fox movie flashed through her mind. The imagery wasn't that far off considering the way her legs had looked the day before.

Clara ducked behind the counter to rifle through the lost and found once again, but came up with nothing. She spotted a set of winter gloves. They'd be useful. And it was likely they'd been sitting here waiting to be claimed since last winter. But she couldn't bring herself to grab them. The guilty sensation she was normally able to push aside niggled at her chest, pressing its ugly face against the window of her soul.

How many things were in that book of hers? How many times had she taken what didn't belong to her in the name of survival. It wasn't right. She'd *chosen* the woods. Chosen to separate herself from society. To live off the land, free of the eyes of people. But who was she kidding? She wasn't living off the land. She was living off other people, haunting them as surely as a ghost trapped in their attic.

Shame filled her until her cheeks were hot with it.

She shoved the gloves back in the basket, hating that she couldn't take something she needed, hating that she needed to take them in the first place.

Hating herself for being so weak she'd run away from her problems and pain in the first place.

She clenched her teeth together, willing herself not to cry.

The kitchen. She'd been on her way to check the kitchen. She'd noticed a desk in the corner with note pads and menus. It was obviously where the cook planned his meals. Perhaps he'd left her notebook there, among the others.

Clara went through the dining room this time instead of directly into the kitchen. It was smart to never take the same way in. Change things up.

The room was empty and dark, so she ghosted past the tables and sidled up to the swinging doors that separated the dining area from the kitchen. Her hand caught in a fake cobweb and she jumped at the feel of the sticky strings in her fingers.

Shaking free of the decoration, she peeked through the window in the door. The kitchen was empty, with only one row of lights on. She watched for several minutes just to make sure, but there was no one else around. Cautiously, she pushed through the door, blinking against the brighter light. Zeroing in on the desk in the corner, she started for it, but her eyes caught on the prep counter and she stalled.

Several containers of food sat tempting her, but what pulled her forward wasn't the smell of savory beef. It was the scrap of paper sitting next to it. Old, and with pink lines instead of the usual blue. It was from her lost book.

With shaking hands, she reached for it, eyes tumbling over the scrawled words written there.

Write down what you need and I'll get it for you. But you have to quit stealing from us or I won't be able to help you.

Clara's throat burned with the threat of unshed tears. *Help you.* The cook wanted to help her? Or was this a trap?

She looked at all the food he'd left. She let the note fall to the counter and wrapped her hands around the foam cup. Whatever was inside was still warm. She lifted the lid, holding the steaming drink to her nose. Hot chocolate. With cinnamon like her abuela used to make.

She choked up. He'd made her food. She'd stolen from him, stolen from many, and when he'd caught her, he didn't shun her or turn her in. He'd made her food. And it was clear he'd read her book. He knew how awful she was. How many things she'd taken. But instead of judgment, this man had chosen kindness.

Her hand went to her chest, pressing against the sharp pain there. It wasn't the first time someone had extended kindness to her when she didn't deserve it. Forgiveness when retribution was what she deserved. And just like the last time, she wanted to run from it.

But she couldn't. Not until she got her book back. It was the one thing that made her a little less of a monster.

On shaking legs, Clara went to the desk for a pen and scribbled her own note on the back of the paper. Then she double checked the dining room and the freezers to make sure she was alone.

With tears in her eyes, standing near the exit in case she needed to run, she ate the food he'd prepared for her.

The stew was hearty, the meat tender and the sauce, seasoned perfectly. The biscuits crumbled when she bit into them, the flavor of sharp cheese and garlic singing along her taste buds. It was the best meal she'd eaten in six years, made even better by the kindness behind the gesture. As long as she lived, she'd never forget this. She tucked the dessert in her backpack and carried the remaining hot chocolate out with her.

She walked right out the front door, not caring about the cameras or if her scent, which she hadn't bothered to hide, gave her away. She was as good as caught anyway. If not by the authorities, then by the compassion shown to her by a perfect stranger she'd done wrong.

This time, it wasn't someone else's sins she had to account for. It was her own. And the only way to do it, was to let this play out.

Fear was her shadow as she made her way back to the deep woods.

***

Eagan was up before the sun. The benefits of not being able to sleep. He'd tossed in his bed most of the night, his thoughts on the female. He'd wonder if she returned. If she found the food he'd left her. Wondered where she slept, if she was warm enough.

His jag had harassed him to come wait for her. Catch her so they could get their questions answered. So he could scent her properly and determine what kind of threat she was.

But he'd held back. Fought whatever strange instinct his cat felt for the female.

Awareness niggled at the back of his mind. Something he desperately wanted to be wrong about. But what were the chances this thief was his mate? It would be the sorriest trick fate ever pulled. To bring her here, when he purposely hadn't sought her out. When he couldn't have her. Wouldn't.

When it was finally close enough to sunup, he quickly showered and dressed. Locking up his cabin, he took his four wheeler through the dark and winding roads that separated the lodge from the cats' homes.

Nobody was up yet, or if they were, they were being as quiet as he was.

In the lobby, he gave Count Dracula a knock on the noggin to wake him up.

"Muuu-ah-ah-ah. Velcome to my castle. Care for a bite?"

"Not today, man," Eagan breathed in good humor.

His steps took him quickly to the kitchen. As soon as he was through the doors, his nose perked up. He stopped, inhaling deep to imprint the scent that slammed into his sternum. His eyes fell closed and his muscles went limp, his jaguar reacting in a way he'd never experienced before.

Lavender and the green of the spruce trees. And something else. *Woman*. Hot, wild woman. His woman. *His.*

Eagan's breath rushed in and out of his chest, making his nostrils flare. His cat lit into a purr that rumbled the air in the room.

He stalked forward, eyes on the counter. There was nothing left of the food he'd intended for her and that settled his animal some. But on the counter was the piece of paper from her notebook. He lifted it to his nose, inhaling deep. She'd inadvertently left her scent there. Lotion perhaps. But for sure, she'd skipped the hunting attractant this time.

A sly smile curved his lips. Finally, her scent. He could track her now. And he would. Because she was his. This scent proved it.

His mate.

He'd vowed to never search for his intended. He'd made the pact with his clan like everyone else. No mating. Protect the females by abstaining from the mating bond. Magic's law. The clan's law. *His* law.

But she'd found him, and under the most unlikely circumstances. This was fate in action.

How could anyone argue against fate?

His grin faded as he lowered the paper.

Magic was going to be pissed when he found out. He'd lose his shit over this, for sure.

Eagan clenched his jaw, thinking.

She'd left her scent, which meant he could track her... and so could anyone else. Magic for example. Or Gash, if he caught her scent where it wasn't supposed to be on a security run. Right now, it was fine. Her scent would mingle with the other humans at the lodge, but if she returned... if her scent was discovered where items went missing...

Eagan's eyes flew across the words she'd left him.

Please, I need my notebook back. If you return it, I swear I'll never come back here again.

In theory, that was exactly what needed to happen. If she kept coming around, she'd be caught. But reality was a bitch, because Eagan couldn't let her get lost in the woods, never to be seen again. He couldn't go sleepless at night wondering if she was okay, if she had what she needed, if she was taking other people's hard earned things. It was clear she regretted her actions. Was he supposed to let her keep doing them?

He frowned, his heart crashing against his ribcage.

He couldn't have her. Magic would never allow it. But he *needed* to be sure she was safe and no longer homeless.

Bailey burst through the doors, and Eagan quickly shoved the note in his pocket.

"Oh, hey. Morning, boss."

"Morning, Bailey."

"You're here early."

"Yeah. Uh, busy day ahead, you know." Eagan shrugged off his jacket and reached for his apron.

He was going to deal with his mate later, but for now, he had to go about his duties. Any deviation would catch Magic's attention. And tonight was the long awaited kick-off of their weekly campfire stories. People would be coming in from the neighboring town of Weston to hear Gash tell spooky tales about the woods. All in preparation for Halloween week when they'd turn those woods into a haunted attraction for their guests. It was a short and sweet celebration, unlike their massive month-long Christmas one, and a much needed break from the preparations for it. Magic said they'd be all out of Christmas spirit if they didn't have a break. Thus The Haunting at Lake Haven was born.

Eagan loved the way the cats celebrated holidays, but today, he wished he could set it aside.

He inhaled again. One last stroke of her scent before they began cooking, and all traces of her were gone.

Forget creepy campfire stories. He had his own ghost to find.

SEVEN

"They call her the Woman of the Woods. The Lady of Lake Haven. Wild hair, black as night. Skin, translucent as an angel's..." Gash spoke in a low, wary tone. He wasn't animated like you'd expect him to be, telling a group gathered around the blazing fire a ghost story. Which actually made it all the more scarier. Made it seem real. "Or a demon's," he said, peering distractedly off into the darkness of the trees.

Eagan leaned against the trunk of an oak and crossed his arms over his chest. The man was good. He'd give him that. The jagged claw mark down Gash's left cheek made him the perfect person for the job of story teller. But every time he described the woman who supposedly haunted the woods of the lake, Eagan couldn't help thinking of his thief.

"By way of magic, she can sneak into any house, through any locked door or window." He lowered his voice to a dead whisper. "Nothing can keep her out. Not an ADT special. Not even the prayers of your great Aunt Susie who's tight with Jesus, like this." Gash held up his hand, two fingers crossed, for emphasis. "And when she doesn't want to be seen, she won't. And when she does... well, you should watch out, because the lady will be the last thing you ever see."

Murmurs sifted through the crowd, eyes darting to the dark trees and back to the fire as Gash continued.

"She takes what she wants from you and then, when she has it all, when you have nothing else to offer, when your very existence is the only thing left..." He closed his eyes, his voice going monotone with dread. "She takes your *soul*. Right to hell with her. Where she keeps it forever and ever."

Goddamn.

Eagan looked around, hoping the kids didn't have nightmares tonight.

"Alright," Magic boomed, clapping his hands together. "We have hot chocolate and cookies, right over there. Help yourselves."

"But don't go too close to the woods," Gash warned, never breaking character.

Eagan watched over the drink and cookie supply in case they needed refilling, barely restraining himself from throwing the cookies at people so they'd leave faster.

Gash came to stand beside him, his eyes trained on Bailey as she served hot chocolate.

"Good story," Eagan murmured.

Gash smirked. "You like that? It's a modified version of the truth."

"What truth?"

Gash stared at him. "Don't tell me you've

never heard about the Woman of the Woods."

Eagan raised an impatient eyebrow.

The cat shook his head, exasperated. "I keep telling Magic, but he won't listen. She's haunting the lodge."

Eagan let out a skeptical chortle. "You believe in all that?"

Gash blinked like he was stupid. "No, asshole, not the soul stealing shit. The Woman in the Woods is a legend. Not of the supernatural variety either. She's a thief known for being practically invisible. There's hardly a home or business in the lake area that hasn't been her victim, but she's uncatchable. Nobody's ever seen her. Only felt the fear she instills. Some actually believe she's a ghost."

Eagan went cold. Mother of fuck, his woman was a legend. And not the good kind.

"A woman, huh?"

"The only reason the locals believe she's a woman is because she's taken beauty supplies and shit. I personally think it's a couple. A man and a woman."

Eagan jerked his head. "What makes you think that?"

Did his female have a man? Shit. Fucking shit.

Hellllll no. That would not stand.

Gash shrugged and Eagan struggled not to take him by the throat and wrangle all his secrets from him. "I dunno. Just seems like too much for one person to pull off."

"But why do you think it's a man?" Eagan ground out.

Gash frowned, staring at him with narrowed eyes. Then he laughed. "A woman couldn't go that long without getting caught. No fucking way."

Eagan caught Bailey's glare. If Gash kept talking like that, he wouldn't last long in their clan. There were too many strong females. And too many males that respected them.

He stepped closer to the cat. "I bet a woman gave you that." Eagan gestured to Gash's cheek and he stiffened. "Word to the wise, you'll catch more females if you drop the sexist bullshit."

Eagan tipped his head toward Bailey, and Gash's shoulders slumped.

Picking up the empty cookie trays, he pushed past Gash and headed for the lodge. He had a meal to prepare.

After considering his options all day, he'd realized he couldn't just hunt his female down like he wanted. For one, it would probably scare her and send her farther into the woods. For two, it would get his animal amped up and wanting to mate. And that was unacceptable.

He had to think of the pact, of his clan, but he also had to think of her. He wouldn't harm her by claiming her. He wouldn't cause her more trouble than what she already dealt with. He'd protect her. And stay good and far away.

Eagan shoved the dirty trays into the wash sink, and gathered the ingredients for his mate's meal. Dinner for his clan and their guests had been grilled chicken and salmon, which didn't make for a good reheat, so he was going to make her something fresh. He was practically famous for his pasta concoctions. He'd keep it simple tonight. Alfredo with sun-dried tomatoes and chicken.

He bit his lip.

Did she like white sauce? In his experience, most people liked pasta. And most preferred a cheesy sauce. Maybe his female was the exception though.

Damn it. He knew so little about her.

He shook his head and got to work filling a pot with water and chopping the leftover chicken into thin strips. He functioned like a well-oiled machine. The kitchen was really just an extension of his soul as he poured himself into preparing food that would fill his female's belly. The idea that she would eat something he'd made her, and it'd keep her full through the night made him practically glow with pride.

When he was plating the dish, his phone rang. He juggled the hot pan and pasta fork back to the counter and then fished his cell phone out of his pocket.

Magic's number flashed on the screen.

"Yeah," Eagan answered.

"You busy?"

"Almost done. What's up?"

Magic's tone was some weird cross between jovial and furious. "Come to my office. I have something to show you."

His words set Eagan's scruff to tingling.

"Give me a minute."

"Yeah, hurry." The line went dead.

There was no reason to believe Magic's call had anything to do with his mate, but without knowing her whereabouts—or anything at all about her—he couldn't shed the feeling of dread.

He finished packaging her food and then filled a cup with their special harvest sweet tea and a chunk of lemon.

Eagan sighed. It wasn't enough, but it would have to do.

Pulling her notebook from his back pocket, he jotted her a new note.

I can't return your book. I promise not to turn

you in to the authorities as long as you promise to stop stealing. I will get you anything you need. Make a list. I'll keep the book as assurance.

Quickly, he shoved the dirty dishes in the washer and started it up. Then he turned off the main lights and hurried to Magic's office.

He found his leader and Gash huddled over his computer monitor.

"I think we caught her this time," Magic murmured, his squinting eyes never leaving the screen.

Eagan's steps faltered. They said *her*. Not him. Not them. Her.

Gash nodded his head, grinning. "Run it back again."

Eagan rushed forward to see the video they were reviewing. A woman wearing jeans and a dark shirt showed through the grainy footage as she walked quickly away from the lodge and disappeared into the line of trees that bordered the parking lot. Her hair was down and flowing freely this time, but there was no doubt this was the female he'd caught in the kitchen.

"When was this?" Eagan asked, his eyes taking in every blurry feature. There wasn't much of her face. Just a brief glimpse of her profile. Magic and Gash would never be able to pick her out of a line-up.

"Last night," Gash said.

"Anything go missing?" *Please say no*.

Magic frowned, finally pulling his gaze away from the screen. "No, actually. Nothing."

Eagan sighed in relief. "Then maybe this isn't our thief after all. I mean, obviously if this is her, and she was here last night, she would've taken something. Don't you think?"

"Whatever, man," Gash scoffed. "This is the Woman of the Woods. Layna doesn't recognize her as a guest, and you *know* she never forgets a face."

Eagan shrugged, trying for nonchalance. "Maybe she's here with someone else. An overnight guest. Layna doesn't keep track of who our visitors are fucking does she?"

Gash looked to Magic, who seemed to be contemplating the situation.

"So why was she rushing out to the woods?" Gash blurted, throwing his hands in the air.

"How the fuck would I know?" Eagan laughed. "I'm just saying, this isn't evidence. Especially since nothing was taken from the lodge last night."

"The camera didn't catch her returning from the woods," Magic argued. But it was half-hearted.

Eagan shrugged. "Probably came back another way. Look, we can't be getting all up people's asses in our quest to find whoever's taking shit. People come here expecting a modicum of privacy. We start monitoring their every move, that'll be as bad for business as a thief."

His heart pounded in his chest and he hoped the others couldn't hear it. His logic was sound, but still, it stung him to be leading his brothers in the wrong direction on purpose.

Magic sighed, yanking his floppy man-bun

down and redoing it. When it sat tight atop his head again, he muttered, "Eagan's right. Shit."

Gash nodded reluctantly. "But I have a feeling about this. Something isn't right about this female."

Eagan ground his molars at the cat's impression of his mate.

"Fucking hell," Magic grumbled. "I guess it's time to start patrolling. If the cameras can't do the job, then we'll have to."

"You mean night security?" Gash asked. "Should we hire someone?"

Magic shook his head. "No. We do this ourselves. Can't bring anyone else in on this. We have our secret to protect. It would be hard to do that with an outsider. Besides, we don't know how much this thief knows about us."

Gash nodded.

"I'll take the first watch. Tonight. We'll take turns. I'll get Renner and Owyn to help."

"And Mason," Eagan added. The cat was too mellow for his own good, but Eagan knew he wouldn't hurt the female if he caught her. If it came to that. Which it wouldn't because he was going to catch her himself.

Magic tipped his head. "Keep your eyes peeled and your noses scenting. We'll find this person. And when we do…" He ended with a growl that left chills on the back of Eagan's neck.

But they wouldn't learn of her. Not if he had anything to do with it. Because somehow, he was going to stop her. Somehow he was going to save her. And he was going to do it without mating her.

Somehow.

EIGHT

Clara read the words over and over again. The cook wasn't giving her book back. Not without a fight. But she didn't want to fight him. She stared at the food he'd left for her. *Again*. What did it mean, him feeding her like this? Once was charity, which she both appreciated and loathed. But twice? Twice was something else.

Maybe he was worried she knew he turned into a cat. Did she still believe what she saw in the woods?

Clara crumpled the note into a ball and went to toss it away, but stopped. Instead, she smoothed it back out and stuffed it in her pocket to keep.

Glancing around the empty kitchen, she contemplated her next move. She really didn't want to do this, but she didn't see another way.

Her shoulders sank with defeat. She was going to fight. Fight the kind man who would feed her instead of turn her over to the police.

Yeah. This was the only way to get back what was hers.

"Be strong, Clara," she whispered. "Be tough. Be the badass you've always wanted to be. You can do this."

With a deep breath, she rushed over to his desk. She had to find something of his. Something important. Some that proved he was supernatural. Mythical even. Something to hold for ransom.

She'd start here, and if she didn't find anything, she'd locate his room. Tear it apart until she had him by the balls. He'd give her book back then. He'd have to unless he wanted it to be front page news that cat-men existed in the Ouachitas.

She rummaged through the drawers, not bothering to keep quiet. There was no one around. If he'd meant to catch her, he would've done it already. With her hip, she shoved the drawer closed to move on to the next one. She might be thinner than before, but her hips were still broad, and they sent the drawer soaring home with a loud slam.

Shit.

She hesitated for only a second before she began shuffling through the next drawer. There were papers galore, pens and markers, rubber bands, but nothing personal. Nothing that she could use against him.

Clara yelped as a heavy hand wrapped around her mouth from behind.

"Shhh," a voice hissed at her ear. "You have to trust me right now, okay?"

He didn't wait for her to respond. With his other hand, he reached forward, sweeping his arm along the surface of the desk and knocking everything to the floor. In a swift move, he twisted her until she was facing him, and lifted her to sit on the desk like she weighed no more than a feather.

"Wrap your legs around me," he urged.

Clara barely found his face for the way her head was spinning. It was her cook. His dark brows furrowed over slate gray eyes. His expression was urgent, demanding. What was happening? She was caught, she knew that much. But what the hell?

"Do it." He shot a look over his shoulder to the door. "He's coming. Follow my lead."

Grabbing her legs behind the knees, he pulled them up around his hips, and for some reason, she did exactly what he'd told her, locking her heels in place. Like this, they were too close. Too intimate. The hard planes of his abs pressed against her stomach, stealing her breath. His steely arms banded around her waist, pulling her in even closer until there was only a breath separating them.

Touching. They were touching. She was touching another human being. Something she hadn't done in ages.

Her breath came stiffly. Too much. Too little. Too much...

He touched her face. So carefully, even though the rest of his actions were urgent and rushed. His thumb was a gentle graze against her skin, lulling her into a calmness she'd never felt with another.

"Shit," he said under his breath, his eyes closing for a moment. When they opened, he looked resigned. "I'm sorry."

Clara tried to find her voice. "For wha—"

His lips crashed down on hers, cutting off her rasped question. They were firm and demanding, and hers gave way to his easily. His hot tongue swept inside her mouth like he was trying to taste her, and the sensation was so decadent, she didn't even try to fight. Hand under her jaw, he angled her head so he could push in farther, bending her backward over the desk.

She'd never been kissed like this. Not ever.

Sure there had been lovers before she'd taken to the woods. Several. But none of them had ever kissed her like they needed to consume her to survive. Like she was simply... *everything*.

An all-consuming fire licked from their point of connection to her middle, causing her toes to curl. She was melting, melting...

The door to the kitchen swung open with a bang and Clara tried to pull away, but her cook held her steady against his working lips.

An agitated throat cleared, and he lazily broke their kiss, sucking at her lower lip on his way back. His gaze burned into her, eyes swirling with emotion she couldn't read. He seemed to promise her something with just that look.

"Go away," he growled, and she jumped at his sharp tone. But his eyes softened, and she could feel his thumb sweeping a soothing pass over the pulse in her neck.

"Like hell," the man at the door seethed. She couldn't see him, but she knew he was angry. "What do you think you're doing?"

"What does it look like?" her cook snapped, and then flashed her a warning look. Clara bit her lip as he peered over his shoulder at the other man. "Do you mind?"

"Fuck yes, I mind. The kitchen isn't exactly the place to bone a rando, Eagan. Get a goddamn room."

His grip on her tightened.

"Serious cock block, Magic, I swear to god." He pulled her off the desk and let her slide down his muscular body until she stood on her own shaking legs.

Holy crap. What was happening to her?

"You know," the man said, "I expect this shit from the others. But not from you. Since when do you hook up with guests?"

Eagan kissed her head, his palm on the back, keeping it tucked against his warm chest. God, he smelled good. Something woodsy and dark like leather. And garlic.

"Come on, baby. Let's get out of here." He squeezed her close to his side with one last press against her head. She got the hint. Keep your head down.

She let him walk her toward the door. They were almost free, but then what? What would her cook do to her then?

Clara felt the moment when things changed. The air in the room went utterly still just before it crackled with energy. It reminded her of the atmosphere right before a thunderstorm. Tense with foreboding. Her eyes met the other man's and she saw his face contort with anger.

"Oh, you've *got* to be kidding me," the other man—Magic? Was that his real name?—snarled. His voice was like a roar in her ear even though she was feet away.

Before she could think to run from the danger, Eagan, shoved her backward, behind him.

"What the fuck is this, Eagan? You covering for a *thief*? Someone who stole from your clan? Your *family*?"

"She's not stealing anymore," Eagan spoke carefully, but the muscles of his back were tensed as if waiting to strike. Clara focused on them instead of the way her ears rang with the word *thief.* "Let this go, Magic."

Clara peered around him to look at the other man. He had shoulder length dark hair that hung in his face, causing his dark eyes to look dangerous. He was angry. Maybe even confused.

"Let this go? What is wrong with you?" Magic shook his head, pulling his phone from his pocket.

"Magic. *Stop.*" Eagan seemed to vibrate with fury. The men were like two atoms about to collide into burst of furious energy.

Shit, she was in trouble. If she escaped this, she'd go back to the woods and never come back. She'd forget about her book and making amends and the man who helped her.

"No," Magic barked, shaking his head and pressing the phone to his ear. "I'm calling the others and we're going to deal with her."

"Nobody will deal with her," Eagan roared, stepping forward, his fists clenched. "She's *mine.* That means *I* will deal with her. Only *me.* So put the damn phone away."

Mine? His?

The conversation was like a foreign language, but whatever Eagan said, it worked. Magic slowly pulled the phone away from his ear.

"What do you mean she's yours?"

Yeah. What did that mean?

"She's my mate," Eagan said, not even tripping over the words. "And I'm claiming her."

Ah. This was more of the act. Damn, he was good at this. If it worked, she'd say her thank-you by never coming back to the lodge again.

"You're *what*?" Magic asked, his brows flaring. "What the fuck was that? I think I heard you wrong."

"I'm claiming what's mine," Eagan spoke clearly. "And that means no one touches her. Anyone tries, I shred them."

Magic looked like he'd been slapped, but Eagan hadn't gotten close enough to touch him.

"Bullshit. You won't break the pact."

"You bet your ass I will."

Magic shook his head in disbelief, and then his troubled gaze met hers. "What's she got to say about this? Huh? You ready to let this cat fuck you like some prized pussy?"

Clara gasped.

"She doesn't exactly have a choice does she?" Eagan ground out, and Magic's gaze snapped back to him.

"You can't do that." But those words weren't snarled as the others were, and instead, he looked broken. Crushed, really. For a split second, Clara felt sorry for him.

"Of course I can. I'm a goddamn male werecat. Not only *can I*, I'm *supposed* to. And I will."

The room fell silent. There was only heavy, angry breaths, and Clara's terrified ones.

It was a slow build from broken to shaking with fury, but when Magic reached fury, Clara felt it like an explosion in the room.

"You..." He shook his head, swallowing disgust so he could speak. "You would hurt your female like that?"

"I'm protecting her."

Magic's fists clenched and opened, clenched and opened. "After all these years... I thought I knew you. But you're no better than the other males, the ones we grew up under. You just needed your fucking female to come along and turn you into a monster. You're disgusting. You make me *sick*."

Eagan's jaw ticked with each word, but he never spoke a word to defend himself.

"I want you gone." Magic pointed a threatening finger at him, backing blindly toward the door. "You're done here. Hear me? I want you gone, before I kill you." He looked at Clara and his face flashed between pity and warning. "You better run, little girl. You'd better hide."

With one parting look of disgust at Eagan, Magic disappeared through the door, leaving it swinging on its hinges.

Clara was breathless with the seriousness of his warning. She looked at Eagan. Werecat. Not human. Kind, or not. She didn't know. Couldn't tell. Maybe he was only gaining her trust with his kindness so he could prey on her.

Fuck her like a prized pussy.

Oh, shit.

Fear clawed her throat, strangling her breath.

Run. Hide.

His back was to her. She could run like before. Out the back door. Get lost in the building like before while he chased her outside. Would he fall for that again?

Her eyes fell to his jeans. Something rigid stuck out from the back pocket.

The notebook. Sweet Jesus, it was her notebook.

She saw the path, and how easy it could be. Grab the book, run like hell, reach the creek and swim so he couldn't track her. She could do it.

On the count of three.

One.

Two...

NINE

Eagan stared at the swinging door, his chest aching with regret. Shit, Magic was hurt. He couldn't miss the look in the panther's eye. Fear and disgust and... pain. The two of them were like brothers. For him to think Eagan was a monster who didn't give two shits about his mate's heart was the fucking worst feeling ever.

But it was necessary.

If the clan thought he was going to claim her, they wouldn't hold her accountable for what she'd done. He just needed a little time. He'd find a way for her to work off her debt and then she wouldn't be on the run anymore. Hopefully he could explain things to Magic later, and he'd understand.

Shit, this was bad.

A tug at his back pocket grabbed his attention, and he turned in time to see his little female make a run for the door, notebook in hand.

Ohhhhh, no she wasn't. Not after what he'd just done to cover her ass.

Eagan lunged for her, but she was a hair too quick, pushing through to the dining room. With a growl, he ran after her. She was fast, even with her short legs, but he caught her at the edge of the parking lot, just steps away from the trail that would take him to his cabin.

In one motion, he scooped her up and tossed her over his shoulder, his steps not faltering as he found the dark trail into the woods.

"Put. Me. *Down*." She smacked his back and kicked her feet, but he wasn't deterred. "Help!" she screamed, and his heart lurched.

She actually thought *he* was the threat? If she

only knew.

He swatted her ass hard enough to make her yelp, but not hurt.

"No one's going to help you except me. So stop it."

She went still. "Help me? Is that what this is? Because it doesn't seem like help. It seems like kidnapping."

Her judgmental tone left him smirking. "So what. You're a thief and I'm a kidnapper. Wanna cast the first stone?"

She went limp as he continued down the path, the darkness enveloping them.

"Please. Just let me go and I'll never come back here, okay? I'll go far away. Find some other forest to live in. Just... please."

"No."

"But why not? I promise I won't steal anymore. I'll... I'll..."

"No. I helped you just now, and look what you did. You ran from me."

The idea both turned him on and infuriated

him. It wasn't supposed to be like this. He wasn't supposed to lay claim to her or hurt his clan or any of this shit. He'd just wanted to feed her and keep her safe and somehow help her make restitution for her crimes so she could be at peace.

"He told me to," she grumbled low enough she probably thought Eagan hadn't heard.

"That's because he thinks I'm going to hurt you."

She was quiet for a few steps. "Are you?"

"Have I yet?"

Another long silence.

"No. Not exactly. But what was all that back there?"

Eagan climbed the steps to his cabin, jiggling the handle until the door came open and maneuvered them both through the entryway. He turned with her still over his shoulder, and flipped the deadbolt on the door.

There. She couldn't run now. They'd stay here until he could figure out what to do.

Carefully, he set her on her feet, and her gaze

scanned the area, looking for an out.

"Don't even think about it," Eagan warned. He went window to window checking the locks and securing the blinds. "They caught you on camera. Magic decided we needed night patrols until you were found. But I knew you'd come back tonight. You were about to get caught. I had to make it look like we were just fooling around."

He turned to look at her, his gaze combing from head to toe. She stood stiff as an oak in the middle of his open living/kitchen area. Her hair was wild and messy, hanging low enough to touch her hips.

Damn, she was beautiful. In the roughest way. An uncut diamond. No makeup, flannel shirt, muddy boots.

She wet her lips, and his eyes settled there.

Those lips. My god, he hadn't meant for that to be their first kiss, but hell if he'd regret it. She'd tasted sweet as a summer peach. And the way she'd rolled her tongue against his... he burned at the memory.

He took a deep breath and continued. "But Magic recognized you, and I had to change the game a bit."

"Lie, you mean."

He lifted one shoulder, looking away. "A little." He wished it were true. Wished he could claim her like Renner had done with Bethany.

"Are you really a... cat-man."

Tea. He'd make tea.

He dug in the cabinet for his bags and then set the kettle to boil before he answered her.

"A werecat. A shifter. My animal is a jaguar."

From the corner of his eye, he watched her. She crossed her arms, uncrossed them, crossed them again.

"But all that stuff you said about mating... that wasn't real, right?"

He got out two cups, setting them too hard on the counter.

Damn it.

"My turn to ask questions." He turned to look at her. "What is your name?"

Fuck, this whole ordeal narrowed to a pinpoint of absurdity. He didn't even know her name. He'd seen her, touched her, fed her, helped her escape, *kissed* her, felt deep affection for her... and he didn't even know her goddamn name. His cat was bonding with her and couldn't give a damn what her name was. But Eagan did.

She shifted on her feet. "I shouldn't tell you."

"Yes, you fucking should." Eagan hooked his hands on his hips. "I chose you over my family. The least you can do is tell me your name."

Her brow furrowed.

"That guy, h-he wasn't serious, was he? He wouldn't really kill you over this."

Eagan rubbed his palm over his jaw, the day's growth rasping against his skin. "I don't know," he murmured. "But one thing's for sure, I'm out of my clan."

"Your clan?"

He sighed. "My shifter family. The only family I have. Woman, would you tell me your name already?"

He was dying to know. Now that she was here and they were talking, the information seemed crucial.

"Clara." Her tone was quiet. Barely more than a whisper. "My name is Clara."

"Clara." Eagan let his mouth feel the syllables. It was perfect. His heart thumped at the sound of saying it. "Clara," he whispered again, closing his eyes to savor it.

The kettle's whistle pierced the space of his cabin. Eagan pulled it from the stove and set the tea to steeping.

"Sugar?" he asked.

"Yes, please." That same barely there tone. He didn't like it. He'd rather her be hissy like before when he carried her here.

He brought the cups over to the couch. "Sit," he urged.

Clara looked around his place, but this time he saw the fear in her eyes. She wasn't looking for an escape, she was uncomfortable.

"What is it?"

"You have so many... things," she murmured. "It's stifling."

Eagan followed her gaze around the room. He was a bachelor. Most of his time was spent working. He *didn't* actually have many things. A couch, a bed, some small tables, and a TV/stereo system. That was about it.

"Well, I guess it's fine you don't like it." It wasn't fine at all. He wanted her to like everything about him. "We won't be here long anyway. We'll find some place you're more comfortable." He gestured with one of the tea cups. "Please. Sit."

Clara nodded, but bypassed the sofa, crouching low on the floor instead. Eagan opened his mouth to stop her, then thought better of it. He handed her one of the cups and she settled in, crossing her legs yoga style. Taking a spot on the floor next to her, he sipped his tea.

"Didn't know cats were tea drinkers," she said, staring into her cup.

Eagan shrugged. "We're part human."

She was quiet.

"Why do I get the feeling you already knew about us?"

The corner of her mouth turned up. "I saw you turn. In the woods one time. I wasn't sure though. I thought I was—" She stopped suddenly, as if trying to catch the words before they spilled from her lips.

Her eyes lifted to him, big and beautiful and vulnerable, before glancing away.

"Crazy. You thought you were seeing things."

She nodded, finding something interesting on the rug.

"What's your story, Clara? Why are you alone in these woods, away from your family and friends?"

Gripping the mug like it might jump from her grasp, she took a drink, closing her eyes as she swallowed. He had the urge to reach forward and feel the softness of her cheek again. His jag had lapped that up when they were in the kitchen. Her skin was caramel satin dotted with the faintest freckles.

She lowered the cup to her lap and met his gaze. "I doubt you'd understand my reasons."

"I still want to know them."

Shaking her head in frustration, she set the tea cup on the floor. "How long are you going to keep me here?"

"I don't know. How long is it going to take to pry your secrets from you?"

She narrowed her eyes at him. "Forever."

"I'll keep you forever then."

Yeah, that sounded right. She was his, and what had he done so wrong anyway? He'd hurt his clan, but he could fix it. Let Magic sleep on it, and they'd talk in the morning. He was a male protecting his female. His leader would understand that. He'd explain to Magic that he planned on wooing Clara the way Renner had done Bethany.

And she'd be the only one for him. Ever. That was what he longed for. What Tana had, what Renner had.

Besides, he knew his mate's heart was tender,

had witnessed it through her notebook. He wouldn't hurt her. Would never.

But maybe... maybe he would keep her.

If he was lucky.

TEN

Eagan rummaged through his dresser drawers until he found his favorite pair of ratty sweatpants. They weren't pretty, but they sure as hell were comfortable. The material was worn and soft.

And pretty much thread-bare in the ass. Which he was *really* going to appreciate once his mate was dressed in them.

In the next drawer, he found the faded out Def Leppard shirt. If she didn't feel comfortable in these, there was no hope for her.

"I told you. I don't need your clothes. I can

sleep perfectly fine in what I have on." She stood near the bathroom, her head tipped to one side in exasperation.

"You'll feel better if you're clean and in something comfortable." He smirked. "Unless you want to try for total comfort and go naked. I'd be okay with that."

Clara rolled her eyes, and it was the sexiest thing he'd ever witnessed. "Are you saying I need a bath? You know, just because I live in the woods, doesn't mean I'm not clean."

He knew she was clean. She smelled too good. She might be a mountain woman, but she didn't have mud on her face or black teeth. Well, there was that one time. But he had a feeling that had all been part of her ruse.

"You're clean enough. But a warm shower and something softer than jeans and flannel will help you sleep better."

She crossed her arms looking defensive. "Why do you care if I sleep? You going to eat me or something. Do cat-men eat people?"

Eagan stepped closer, invading her space. "Do you really think I'd hurt you, Clara?"

She blinked at his nearness.

"I couldn't. Even if I wanted to. If I was the boogey man you believe me to be, I still wouldn't. I couldn't."

"Why couldn't you?"

Slowly, carefully, he reached a hand to her cheek. She stiffened, but didn't pull away. And when his thumb brushed the skin there, she relaxed. His jaguar was so deeply satisfied at her response, he nearly let a purr slip out.

"What I told Magic about you being my mate?"

She nodded, her mouth open on a pant.

"That wasn't a lie."

Her eyes went wide, but she still didn't pull away from his touch. "I don't know what that means," she whispered.

"I know. And we won't talk about it tonight. But just know that I'll always want to protect you. Never hurt you. You're safe with me."

"Safe."

Eagan nodded. He hoped that was true. It felt true. Deep in his heart, he knew he couldn't hurt her.

"I've never been safe," she mumbled softly, like she was testing the idea out loud.

He frowned at her admission, but then she blinked, turning her face away and breaking whatever spell he had on her.

"Fine. I'll shower and wear your clothes if it'll make you happy."

Her lower lip pushed out in a pout as she started to kick off her boots, and he pressed his own lips together so he wouldn't smile.

"Good. And I'll wash those so you can have fresh clothes in the morning."

She tossed him a look that implied washing clothes after one wear was an extravagance she had no tolerance for.

"No need. I have others at my..." She lowered her eyes. "...place. And I can wash these when I go back."

Eagan ignored the 'go back' part. "I'm washing them."

She raised an eyebrow as she began unbuttoning her shirt. "Fine. You want to waste water, that's your business."

But her words were like vapor. They disappeared before they reached his ears, because all his senses were zeroed in on her slender fingers working the buttons from collar to hem.

"What..." Eagan cleared his throat. "What are you doing?"

She frowned. "Giving you my clothes."

"Right. Carry on then."

Carelessly, she parted the flaps of her shirt and began shrugging out of it.

"Shit," Eagan cursed, turning his head. She was completely naked under that shirt. No bra. And the most perfect tits, if he could judge by his half second view of them.

"What?"

He forced his gaze back to her... face. Her face.

Not tits. Face. It was scrunched in confusion.

"What's wrong?"

"You're... you..." He gestured to her topless state, but his eyes roamed and the result was him, speechless.

She was a goddess. Graceful shoulders framed full breasts with dark, perky tips.

Frowning deeper, she tipped her head to the side, her wild hair dancing at her jean clad hip. "Are you the modest type?"

"Uh..." Eagan blew out a breath and rubbed his palm through his hair. "Not exactly."

"These?" she asked, skeptical, grabbing her twin peaks with both hands and holding them like they were just any old part of her body. "At base, they're more functional than sexual. They're basically just feeding bags for when I have a baby."

Eagan's eyebrows shot up and he coughed to cover his surprise. "At base."

She nodded. "Yeah. At their most basic. When you think about the natural way of things, everything becomes really simple. Like early humans. Everything they were made up of had a purpose: to ensure survival. Their strengths, their intelligence. Their bodies and what they did with them. If they killed, they used the whole animal. Nothing was wasted. The same with intangible things like time and love. They lived every minute to the fullest and loved with the most basic of urges. It really makes so much sense if you think about it."

Functional, not sexual. Yeah, tell his raging hard-on that.

"You... you really think your body isn't sexual?"

She shrugged one shoulder, hands still cradling her full breasts. "Sure, it's sexual I guess, somewhat. It can be a little of both if you're talking about perpetuating the race. But then, still, it's really just functional isn't it?"

He stared at her, his eyes sliding to the indention of her waist and her hips that flared wide. Her body was perfect for perpetuating the race, as she put it. His dream of putting a baby into his mate resurfaced. What a thrill it would be to have her with young. *His* young.

But hell if that was all her body was used for. It was made for so much more. It was made for pleasure. To receive it. To give it. To *live* it.

A new dream emerged. To have his mate *living* in pleasure. So sensitive to him and his touch that a mere breath against her skin made her hot. The things he'd do to that body. Completely non-functional things.

His jag purred in agreement.

She dropped her hands, causing her breasts to bounce from the sudden lack of support.

"But if it bothers you, I can shut the door."

Bother him. Fuck no, it wasn't *bothering* him. It was only making him burn below the belt like Satan had him by the balls.

Eagan managed a casual shrug. "Nah. It ain't bothering me. My cat is just shredding my insides because it wants out for a taste of those hard *functional* nipples. That's all."

She gasped, her eyes going wide.

"Yeah. So, I dunno, maybe hurry it on up before things take a turn for the less functional."

Quickly, she undid the button of her jeans. "Does it hurt?"

"What?"

"Your… cat."

Eagan's chest tightened knowing she was concerned. It was sweet. "Not really. But he usually gets what he wants."

She hooked her thumbs in her waistband and pushed her jeans to the floor.

Fucking hell.

Fucking *functional* hell.

"No panties," he rasped.

She wasn't wearing any fucking panties. Nothing. Not a single fucking thing on her curvy hips. Eagan's gaze took her in, not even bothering to fight it this time. Her legs were smooth and luscious, but a wild triangle of hair caught him off guard. Everyone was so well groomed these days, it was almost a shock to see what he assumed was six years worth of hair-down-there. But fuck him... fuck him hard... it was *hot*.

He brushed his fingers over his lips, grappling for control.

"I quit wearing panties years ago." She stepped out of her jeans and bent to pick them up.

Eagan blinked. Damn, she was so feral. So wild. He was the shifter. He was supposed to be the wilder one. But no, this female with her outrageous body and her simplistic approach to life... she was the most straightforward, untamed, thing he'd ever encountered. How did a human best him at being feral? And why the hell was that so irresistible?

She handed him her clothes, and it was a damn miracle he was able to take them without grabbing her and pulling her against his body like he so wanted to.

"I'll just be a few minutes," she said, starting to close the door. He smacked his palm against it to stop her.

"Take more than a few minutes." His voice

was tight. "I need some time."

Her brow furrowed in concern. "Okay."

His breath heaved as the door clicked closed. He stood there, listening as the water kicked on. The cat prowled inside. Mate was so close. Naked with the water rolling over her delectable body.

Eagan spun on his heel, marching through the kitchen area to the washing machine. He tossed Clara's clothes in and added soap. He'd wait to start it until her shower was finished.

He turned, propping his hands on the edge of the washer, breathing deep. There was no hope his erection was deflating. His pants were so tight he might have to cut them off.

An ironic laugh escaped him. How their forefathers did it was beyond him. How they found any female more desirable than their mate. How they could stomach ever being with another. The way he felt about the female in his shower... the bond he felt for her was the most powerful thing he'd ever experienced.

Maybe Renner was right after all. Maybe it

was only a state of mind, and their instincts could be overridden by choice. Maybe you chose who you wanted to be, what kind of love story you wanted to live.

If it was true, if it was a choice… he chose her. Clara. Just Clara. For life.

His sweet and sassy Clara, who'd made mistakes but wanted to fix them. He'd take her forever and make her so happy she'd never want to get lost in the woods again.

Closing his eyes, he tipped his head back on his shoulders, a grin curving his lips.

Functional. He'd show her functional.

ELEVEN

Clara tried to take her time. She really did. But she had a feeling it wasn't enough.

Her circumstances weren't anything she'd ever imagined for herself. Trapped indoors with a paranormal creature. His apparent mate, whatever the hell that entailed. And many years of possible jail time nipping at her heels. The wild part of her kept looking for chances to escape back to her camp. To her skink. To anything that was her own. But the rational side, the thinking, planning, logical side of her knew the truth. That from the moment she'd lost her book to Eagan, her days of freedom were numbered.

All she could do now was ride this out.

And maybe... just maybe she was ready for a change.

When she'd taken to the woods so long ago, she'd had no plan. No time limit for how long she planned on being gone. She'd told her sister not to look for her. Maybe she'd listened, maybe she hadn't. There was no way of knowing. But she'd had her own family to take care of. A husband and two small children.

Clara let herself wonder about them. Wonder how they had handled the same tragedy that sent her running. How had they coped?

She always tried hard not to think of her past. It wasn't welcome in her woods. But technically, she wasn't there anymore. And those memories had a wicked way of forcing themselves on her no matter how hard she fought them.

Esther would be eight now, and Hillary, eleven. Almost a teen. She would have missed so much of their childhood. But they were better off not knowing her. Or... at least the person she used to be.

The person who treasured things over truth and honesty. The person who let someone she loved hurt others because she was too distracted to make them stop.

Clara closed her eyes, letting the water hit her face and wash away any tears. She wasn't sure if they were there or not, and she didn't want to know.

Better not to know. Feeling was too hard.

At base, she needed to survive. She did *not* need to feel. And her cook made her do just that, feel things she hadn't imagined ever feeling. That giddy tumbling in your stomach you get before your heart leaps toward another's. The flutter behind your knees when they want to go weak from a simple touch. She'd felt those and more in the last several hours. Tiny miracles she'd treasure later.

She grabbed the disposable razor she'd found in Eagan's cabinet. It felt like hitting the jackpot, finding one that he hadn't used. She didn't even care that it was a man's. A razor was a razor was a razor. And this thing had five blades so it was like, the Lamborghini of razors. Who the hell needed five blades?

She looked down, considering her bush, and amended that.

What *man* needed five blades?

Using Eagan's spicy smelling conditioner as shave cream, she carefully dragged the razor over her legs. But there was hardly anything to remove after her spa clay treatment.

She shivered. *Never again.*

She repeated the process with her underarms and tried to figure out what to do with her bikini area. The cavewoman in her said to leave it. The hair was there for a reason. But maybe a little trim would be a good idea. Who knew when she'd find another razor.

Did they offer razors in prison or was that something you had to buy with the three cents you got for making license plates or whatever?

She started at the crease of her thigh and worked inward, but it was less shaving and more hacking away, machete in the brush style. Eagan's Lamborghini razor wasn't cutting it.

Clara sighed. A slight culling would have to do.

She turned off the water and dried her body with his too-soft towels. She'd miss sun-drying. Bathing in the hot springs. Even that harsh unscented soap.

Quickly, she dressed in Eagan's clothes. He was right, the fabric was much softer than her jeans and flannel. At one time she'd have considered it comfortable. But now she was used to rough and tough. She had calluses. Plenty on the outside. And not as many as she'd hoped for on the inside.

In the cabinet, she found mouthwash. She rinsed and gargled. It was the best she could do with her toothbrush being back at camp.

With a deep breath, she opened the door and stepped into the main room. Eagan stood at the bed, fluffing a pillow.

"Feel better?" he asked, not looking at her.

"A little. You?" She glanced at his hips to get her point across.

He found her eyes, smirking. "You think you're funny, don't you?"

She shrugged. "It's okay, you know. Masturbating is perfectly normal. Functional even."

His jaw opened in surprise. Why did he always look like that with her? What she'd said wasn't *that* weird.

Unless...

"Or maybe cat-men don't masturbate? I-I don't know how all that works for you. I just assumed—"

"It works the same," he blurted.

She shrugged. "Okay then."

He tossed the fluffed pillow to the bed.

"I didn't masturbate."

"Oh. Well. You know... not my business really. You said you needed time so I thought..."

Eagan closed his eyes as if his head hurt. "Dear god, woman. Can we stop with the sex talk?"

She wanted to laugh. He was strong and gorgeous and he probably had women often, but he came off like a prude.

Clara frowned. *Did* he have women often? The thought bothered her. If she was his mate and all, it seemed like something she should know about him.

"Aren't you a sexual person, Eagan?"

He froze but then answered her. "More than you know, little woman."

So he did have sex. He just didn't like to talk about it.

A kernel of jealousy niggled at her.

"And right now every word out of your mouth is like a stroke to my cock. Get in bed," he commanded.

"We aren't sleeping together."

"Oh, yes we are. It's the only way we're sleeping. I'm not letting you out of my reach so you can escape me. We have shit to work out in the morning, but for tonight, this is what's happening."

Clara eyed him. Something told her she wasn't getting out of this. She glanced at the bed. The idea of sleeping in a real bed after so long left her uneasy. But after what he'd done in the kitchen to keep her safe...

If what he'd said about being kicked out of his clan was true, then she owed him big time. What kind of man gives up his family to protect a thief? She didn't understand it. But could feel herself warming to him. A heart as giving and kind as her cook's couldn't be ignored. It should be loved and cherished, and even though she might never get the chance to do it, she knew the real deal when she saw it.

His kiss had melted her, and not because of any reasons that were shallow. She'd had her days of shallow. His kiss felt *real*. Authentic and desperate. And it had made her desperate too. It had overridden her fear and awoken something within her.

The part of her that wanted to feel again. Wanted the complications of relationships again.

Eagan was the real deal. The billion dollar, once in a lifetime, never gonna find another like him, deal.

Gingerly she placed one knee on the mattress. It was firm, but still had so much give to it. Inch by inch, she crawled forward, settling on the plush pillow and pulling up the mock fur blanket until it reached her chin.

Eagan stared at her, his expression unreadable.

Then, to her surprise, he began undressing. Slowly, he peeled his shirt up, revealing his rippled abs an inch at a time. His skin was smooth and tan with just a light dusting of hair around his navel. Her eyes snagged on those cords of muscle around his waist forming a cut V to his hips and she licked her lips.

Why was that part of a man so attractive? What function did it serve?

Up and up he went with his shirt until his

strong chest was showing. The muscles of his arms bunched and rippled as he pulled the t-shirt over his head and tossed it to the floor.

Her breath caught. This man, her cook, he was beautiful. Like art you shouldn't touch for fear of ruining it.

He stared at her, his eyes blazing.

Clara swallowed the beat of her heart and managed to conjure words. "What are you doing?"

"What does it look like I'm doing? I'm taking off my clothes."

With rough movements, he undid his belt and then the button of his jeans. He never took his eyes off her as he shoved his pants down and stepped out of them. Before she could look away, he'd yanked his boxers down, adding them to the pile.

He stood there, his eyes lasered on her, his fully erect cock jutting proudly in front of him like it was the bow of Good Ship Eagan. Like the needle on a compass and she was true north. It was huge. And *hard*.

God.

She looked away.

"What's wrong, Clara? This?"

She looked back to find him gripping his erection in a tight fist. He ever so slowly, thrust his hips into it. Once, twice, three times.

"It's just functional, you know. It's basically just a sperm hose for making babies." His voice was low and rough, his words sarcastic but his tone not. It was the sound of a man tangled in need, throwing her words back at her in an effort to prove a point.

She knew that. Of course. But her eyes were riveted as he continued to thrust into his own hand.

"I… I… never said there was no use for sex as pleasure," she muttered, crossing her arms but unable to look away.

"Didn't you? You said our bodies were less sexual and more functional. I tend to disagree."

Okay, she could admit she'd been purposely obtuse earlier. But with the way he was throwing around the word mate, she figured she should remind him of the basics.

He sighed heavily, his mouth hanging open, his face growing red from the pleasure he was obviously feeling. "This feels pretty damn sexual to me."

It did to her too. Watching him was turning her on big time, and it had nothing to do with functional. Desire whipped down her spine, settling in between her legs and tingling until she squirmed.

"Okay, stop already," she blurted.

His hand paused at the head of his erection, and the corner of his lip curved up in a rueful smirk.

"What's the matter, little woman? You need some time?"

Some time. Like he'd needed after she'd undressed.

She met his lust-filled gaze and nodded.

"Good. Because I need a shower." He strolled toward the bathroom, giving her a stellar view of his ass. Twin globes of perfection, with a slight indention in each side. *Hot.*

Clara blew out a breath and fanned her face.

His body was plenty functional. Its function was to make her sweat. And pant. And lust.

"Oh," he added, just before he closed the bathroom door. "I'm going to masturbate now. Thought you should know."

Her jaw hung open and she didn't even try to contain it. The door clicked shut and she threw her head back on the pillow.

How would she ever sleep now? With that vision of Eagan pumping his erection every time she closed her eyes. After six years, she'd thought she was over sex based on lust. Sex based on purpose had a point and fit into her neat little survival criteria. But what she'd just experienced with Eagan—what little she'd just experienced— left her feeling truly wild. Like even the woods didn't make her feel.

What was happening to her?

She should be focusing on escaping. Now was

her perfect chance while he was distracted in the shower. But something told her he'd be on her trail faster than she could say whoa. And besides, in here, with Eagan, she felt safe. Beyond that door somewhere was a very angry werecat named Magic.

No, she'd stay right here, in her cook's bed. It really wasn't such a bad place after all. It smelled like him and was warm. And it made him say dirty things that revved her up.

She wasn't so sure about this mating thing, but sticking close to Eagan—even if it meant getting a little less functional—was something she was on board with. Plus, he challenged her. Made her bolder, even if she was trying to use it as a wall between them. He made her *think*. Maybe that would prove to be devastating. Maybe it wouldn't. But she was ready for that much of a change at least.

Decision made.

***

Eagan could sleep through a lot. Like the

dead, some would say. He was a cat after all, and cats were notorious for sleeping. So all his mate's tossing and turning didn't bother him much. He was aware of it, but it never brought him out of sleep. When she gently touched his shoulder though, that was a different story altogether.

"Wake up," she hissed. Her mouth was close to his ear. He could feel her breath skate across his skin, and it sent all the blood in his body straight to his cock.

He inhaled deeply, her scent invading his nostrils and making him even more hungry for her. His wild little human was divine. And the fact that she wasn't unaffected by him... that was just icing on the cake.

"Eagan." Her whisper broke the silence with another shove to his shoulder.

He rolled onto his back, peeking at her through slitted eyes. "What is it, mate?"

"I can't sleep."

"I noticed," he murmured, reaching through the darkness to touch her cheek.

"Yeah, right," she said, but she leaned her face into his touch. "You were sound asleep. Snoring, in fact."

He grinned. "I wasn't snoring."

Her lips turned up. "You kinda were." She sighed, her smile evaporating. "Can I sleep on you? The bed is too soft and you're obviously hard." Her eyes skimmed his chest.

"You want to sleep on me?" he asked, unsure. "Like a bed?"

Clara nodded. "It's either you or the floor. And I'm thinking you'd be much warmer."

His female wanted to sleep on him. She wanted to use his body for comfort. His heart pounded against his ribs and throat tightened. Her request gave him more joy than she could ever know.

And she was right, he was hard. In the wrong place. His erection throbbed at the mere idea of her on top of his body. She'd surely be even more uncomfortable if she knew.

But how could he tell her no. Those big gold-brown eyes staring at him expectantly, it was impossible.

"Climb up," he rasped.

Her relief was apparent in the way her shoulders went from tense to slack. He held the covers back for her while she slung her leg around his waist to straddle him. When she was maneuvering, he adjusted his erection so it was lying on his belly. Slowly, she lowered her head to his chest, her torso pressing his hardness between their two bodies.

Eagan grit his teeth. He could do this. His mate needed sleep, and he was going to help her get it.

Easing her legs until they lay parallel with his, she let out a sigh and he felt her body relax.

Aw, damn that felt good. His mate's comfort was almost as satisfying as sex might be. And a hell of a lot more satisfying than the palmer he'd given himself in the shower.

He took a deep breath and felt his own body relax. But there was nowhere for his arms.

"Better?" he asked.

She nodded, her curls brushing against his chest. "Much. Am I too heavy?"

"Not a chance. You're perfect like this."

She relaxed a fraction more, making his chest throb with emotions he'd have to deal with come morning.

"Can I put my arms around you? Would that keep you awake?"

She was silent for so long he wondered if she'd already drifted off.

"Go ahead."

Eagan slowly brought his arms up until one was wrapped securely around her waist and the other with his palm between her shoulder blades. She let out another relaxed sigh, and he was struck with the realization that everything was as it should be in that very moment in time. A perfect second in an infinity of seconds.

There wasn't any sacrifice he wouldn't make for her. Nothing was asking too much. His clan, his body, his mind, he'd lose any of it for her. And *that*, he knew instinctually, was what a big cat mating was truly about. The rest of it was just tradition. The ways of their ancestors weren't *their* ways. And the great thing about traditions was they could be broken.

Renner had it right. And Eagan was going to help him show the others.

With that thought settled, sleep pulled at him once again.

"Do you normally sleep in trees?"

"No," Clara murmured drowsily. "A mattress made of a sleeping bag and old newspapers."

His heart squeezed tight at the thought of his mate in the wild, sleeping on scraps she'd collected. Never again. Even if he had to follow her out there and be her personal Tempur-pedic.

He squeezed her tighter against his chest. "Damn. There goes my Katniss fantasy."

"Who?" she asked, her voice slurred with sleep.

He let out a soft laugh. "Nevermind. Sleep, little woman."

TWELVE

Clara was ripped out of the best sleep of her life by a knock on the cabin door. A bang really. Several urgent bangs. Eagan's big hand on her head urged her further from her sweet coveted rest.

She lifted her drowsy eyes to his and her breath caught in her chest. His gaze glowed with emotion so fierce it should have scared her. But it didn't. With his ruffled hair and sleep-sexy face and his strong arms holding her steady, all she could feel was... safe.

She felt safe, and that... was a miracle.

"Someone's at the door," he murmured.

Clara nodded and rolled to the side, back onto the cushy bed. Eagan sat on the edge of the mattress and pulled his pants on over the boxers he'd worn to sleep.

He turned to look at her, his eyes wary. "Stay here. I'll protect you, Clara. Remember that. And whatever happens... do not run from me."

"I won't." She meant it.

He bent slowly, and kissed the top of her head. The gesture was so sweet, so protective, it left her insides quaking. That was her cook, always looking out for her. What had she done to deserve his loyalty? She wanted to be worthy of him, but the truth was he was too good for her.

Eagan edged the door open. "Bethany," he said.

Clara recognized the name. It was the woman from the spa.

"You alone?" Eagan asked.

"Yes. Can I come in?"

He hesitated, but finally flung the door wide

for her to walk through.

"I came to check on your guest," she informed as she made her way toward the couch which sat adjacent to the bed. A single half wall separated the living area and the bedroom. "Hi, there." She smiled brightly as she spotted Clara.

Clara attempted to return it, but it was early, and she hadn't talked to anyone but Eagan in too many years. And the only other person she'd come in contact with wanted to "deal" with her and kill Eagan. So she wasn't exactly ready to buddy up to any of them.

"I see you aren't bound and gagged as Magic might have suggested."

Clara frowned. None of that. Eagan had been a little saucy, but never cruel.

"Fucking kidding me," he muttered, running a hand through his hair. "I wouldn't hurt my mate. I'm not a monster."

Bethany looked at him. "I know. The others too. Nobody believes you're going to mate her."

Eagan stiffened.

"Unless... *are* you going to mate her?"

His eyes flashed to Clara and then to the ground. "What are you doing here, Bethany?"

"Checking on your sweetheart. Like I said. Magic told me she was human, so I thought another human face might cheer her up."

"You're not a cat-woman?" Clara managed.

Bethany's grin was so friendly, Clara relaxed a notch. "Nope. I'm as human as they come." She stepped forward with her hand outstretched. "I'm mated to Renner. He's a cat. Like Eagan. So, I kind of get what you're going through right now. It can be a lot to take in all at once."

Slowly, Clara raised her own hand and gave the woman a single shake before dropping it. "Clara," she murmured.

"Nice to meet you, Clara."

"Did..." Should she ask? Was it too personal? "Did Renner get kicked out when he mated you?" Maybe there was a way back into the fold after the mating was done. Not... not that her and Eagan would mate, but she'd feel better knowing he

157

could be with his family again if he wanted.

Bethany cocked her head to one side, considering the question. "No. But we kind of consider that a Christmas miracle. We definitely broke Magic's rule, but he gave us a pass. I'm sure he has his reasons. He's not usually so... um... riled."

Clara moved to the side of the bed, tossing a glance at Eagan. He stood against the wall with his arms crossed over his chest staring at the floor. She looked at Bethany.

"I don't want to get him in trouble," she said quietly.

She knew he'd hear, but so what. It had been weighing on her conscience ever since he'd thrown her over his shoulder and marched her to his cabin. He felt some obligation to keep her out of trouble. It wasn't fair for him to lose his family over her.

Bethany's lips curled into a sad smile. "Oh, you're special," she whispered. Not in a condescending way. But like she was truly surprised. She turned her attention toward Eagan. "I wonder if there's such a thing as a Halloween miracle?" She raised one eyebrow at him.

"I hope so," he muttered almost to himself, and kicked his foot up on the wall behind him. His stance was casual, but his expression was anything but.

Bethany stepped closer to him, and Clara had the urge to glue herself to his side.

"None of us think you're a monster, Eagan. You just need to explain to them what's happening. Especially Magic. He's taking this hard."

What was happening? Clara wanted to tell them to quit speaking in code and explain this to her.

Eagan nodded. "Yeah. Maybe you're right." His tone didn't sound convinced.

"Bailey's manning the kitchen. Renner and Owyn are talking Magic down. Layna is taking care of business. Everything is going to be fine.

Just... tell him. Tell him what I see here. Make him understand." She hesitated. "Like Renner did."

Eagan gave her another non-committal nod.

Bethany shot Clara an encouraging smile and then strolled to the door. "Tell Clara too, Eagan. Nothing sucks worse than being a human in the dark."

Clara agreed with that statement. Wholeheartedly.

***

The brush was thick this far off the path. It was barely noon and the sun beat through the orange and gold tent of leaves, whisking away the chill of the autumn morning. But the promise of a crisp nightfall was never more than a breath away.

Clara turned right at the rock she'd set for a marker.

Maybe this was a bad idea. Maybe she shouldn't trust him this much yet.

But how could she not? He'd taken care of her, kept her notebook to himself even at the cost of alienating his clan, and when she would have been caught, he'd made a way for her to escape. She had to believe that he was helping her because he saw through all the bad to something good in her. She was his mate, but it had to be more. Had to be, or he wouldn't risk his family. She had to believe she wasn't too far gone.

"Almost there," she called behind her.

After she'd agreed to take him to her camp, Eagan had gone quiet. He seemed lost in thought. But his steps were steady behind hers as they crunched through twigs and fallen leaves.

"You're smart," he murmured. "You picked a good area to hide out in."

"Not hide out," she corrected. "I'm not on the run. Well... I guess I could be if Magic had called the cops."

"I just meant, this is solitary enough no one would happen upon you. Not even one of the cats. We like to stretch our legs in these woods but generally we don't go out this far."

Clara smiled. "You wouldn't have found me

anyway."

Eagan barked out a laugh. "That right?"

"Mm hm. I'm very good at hermitting."

They stopped when they reached a cluster of thick saplings and vines that spanned a twenty foot gap between older trees. Here, the cover was so thick it was almost impossible to see through. Any place thin enough to offer a peek, only revealed rock that bled into the mountain.

"Here we are," she said.

"Here?" His tone was skeptical.

"Yep."

Clara stared up, through the trees to the cliff that peaked a couple hundred feet above her head. The faithful cliff. It had never given away her secrets and now, she was going to do that very thing.

Before the day was over, Eagan would have them all. Somehow, she knew it.

She glanced at him. His hands were slung around his hips as he examined the brush cover, looking for her so-called camp.

"Where?" he asked, baffled.

Clara had to laugh. "Come on."

She led him to the "door". It wasn't really a door, but she liked to think of it as one. It was a spot in the brush wall where several thick vines had grown together. But if you knew just where to separate them, they opened as easily as a door, instead of a snarled tangle of twigs.

Ducking, she crawled through until she was on the other side of the wall. Once past, there was barely enough room to stand between the trees and where the rocky mountain face began.

She glanced back to make sure Eagan had followed her. But he was so close, she startled and her foot caught on a root. Flinging her hand out to find purchase, she grabbed his shirt and his strong hands steadied her. She looked up, expecting to find him scowling, but instead, his eyes were soft, crinkling around the edges. Not laughing at her. Something else.

It gave her a repeat dose of that belly tumbling feeling. It was something she could easily become addicted to.

His gaze fell to her lips and he didn't look away.

Shoved between the rock and the vines, with the tree canopy above them, it was like they were the only two people in the world. It was their own little place in the universe. Until today, it had only been hers. Now it was *theirs*.

It was a scary but exciting feeling, sharing something so important with this man. But he'd made the first move. He'd shared his cooking, his home. His *bed*.

Slowly, Eagan bent his head to hers. Inching forward, as if giving her time to stop him. Except she didn't want to stop him. For once in her life, she craved a connection. She wanted to match a piece of her with a piece of him, and make it mean something.

His lips pressed softly to hers, and the delicate touch might as well have been thunder for the effect it had. It was so sweet, so delicious that it took her breath away. There was no tongue.

No urgency. Just the most tender meeting of his body with hers.

And it undid her.

All the solitude. The simplicity. The distance from society. It seemed like her past, and this, Eagan, was her future.

It scared her. But only in the way of embarking on a new adventure.

It also thrilled her. But in the way a haunted house was thrilling. What surprise was around the next corner? And could she survive it without wetting her damn pants.

His hand tenderly cradled her cheek as he broke their kiss, just enough to speak.

"That was what I wanted our first kiss to be. Gentle, so I could feel how soft your lips are. I knew they'd be the softest." His mouth brushed hers as he spoke sweetly. It might as well have been more kissing since it had the same breath-stealing effect on her.

"It's okay," she whispered, letting her lips caress his too. "I liked them both. And... and I hope there's more."

His eyes closed as he sighed, seeming relieved. She could almost feel it rolling off him.

He kissed the corner of her mouth and pulled back. "Let's see this camp of yours so we can go talk to Magic. I need to get things settled with you or my jag'll go crazy."

Clara breathed deep to get her bearings.

"Yes. Camp. Let's go."

Squeezing along the wall, she led Eagan to a hidden opening in the rock. It was three feet across and almost five feet tall, and covered by a canvas tarp. Pulling it back, she peered inside.

"You got the flashlight?"

Eagan passed it over and she used it to light the inside of the cave.

"There might be critters. They stay away for the most part when I'm here. But being gone overnight... you never know."

She stepped inside and Eagan followed.

Her bed was against the wall. The floor had been swept until only the rock showed. A small container of supplies sat off in the corner. It was where she kept her books and the weather radio for emergencies. In the center of the small space was her tiny fire pit that hadn't been used for most of the summer.

It was simple. Modest. It was home. But for some reason, looking at it now, it seemed... crazy. She could see how a stranger would think she'd lost her marbles.

A burning kernel of embarrassment planted in her gut.

"It's... you know... functional. Not much, but everything I needed."

She couldn't look at Eagan. What if she could tell what he was thinking, and what he was thinking was that she was looney.

"I'm not... crazy. I just take pleasure in the simple things." Tears threatened, but she pushed them back, desperate to retain a shred of dignity. Was it so far out there to want to live with minimal needs? To keep to yourself and revel in the gifts nature granted. Was she... was she nuts for wanting to leave the smallest footprint possible?

"I never said you were crazy. You're more like a shifter than you think, finding your connection with nature. It's really something. And I'm *definitely* concerned about what you take pleasure in." His voice was playful, and a nervous laugh escaped her.

Eagan turned in a circle, taking in the cramped surroundings.

"I love what you've done with the place."

She glanced at him, and he gave her that sarcastic smile.

"Oh, shut up. Your cabin doesn't even have any pictures on the walls." She pointed the flashlight to the other side of the cave. "At least I painted my place." She'd collected whatever leftover paint she could find throughout the years and went caveman on the wall. No hieroglyphs though. Normal stuff like flowers and stars.

"Yeah, yeah. Okay, Martha Stewart." He grinned, winking. But she could've sworn he looked… proud.

Clara shrugged. "I got skills."

He reached for her hand, linking his fingers with hers. "Alright, let's grab the stuff you took from the lodge and get it back to Magic."

"Oh, that. Um, that stuff isn't here."

Eagan frowned. "It's not?"

Clara shook her head. "Hermit 101. Keep your stash away from your camp. That way if either is compromised, you don't lose both in one fell sweep."

He raised an eyebrow. "Huh." Reaching forward, he tweaked her nose. "Then take me to your stash, oh great mountain woman."

Clara grinned. "Fiiiiiine."

***

Eagan carted the plastic tub of supplies on one shoulder and held his mate's hand as they took the path through the woods that would lead them back to the lodge. He was going to talk to Magic. All he could do was try. If the man refused to listen, then he would take Clara and go. They'd make their own way. Without a clan.

If she wanted him.

His stomach knotted at the thought that she might not want to share this life with him. Maybe she wanted to stay in her woods, with her solitude.

Bethany was right. He should tell her. But they were still so new. What if this was all too much too fast?

Her stomach growled.

"I want to make you breakfast," he told her. "Maybe after we talk to Magic."

"I'm okay. I'm used to going longer without food."

His jaw clenched and he had to work to speak. "I don't want that for you anymore."

They walked in silence and he could sense the tornado of thoughts swirling over her head.

"I chose this, you know? Being a mountain woman. I wanted this."

"I know you did. And I get the attraction. But... why? What sent you out there?"

More silence. More thinking. He was patient. He could wait for her to collect her thoughts.

"When I was twenty-one, something bad happened to my family." She paused. "Well, actually, something bad happened *because* of my family. You ever hear of the Destacios?"

Eagan shook his head.

She gave a sideways grin. "Good. Then I traveled far enough away."

He pulled her out of the way of a rock in the path.

"My family was wealthy, rich off the real estate market. My father was the breadwinner, but my mother had the brains. Investing, selling, investing again. They—*we*—were swimming in extravagant crap we didn't need." She smiled. "I remember even as a teenager thinking, this is too much. *So* much. We don't need it." She shook her head. "I was weird even then."

"Not weird," he murmured. His mate wasn't materialistic. There was nothing wrong with that. "Sensible."

"Yeah. Maybe." She sighed, and he squeezed her hand to urge her to continue. "'This money is a poison,' my dad would say, as he spent it on booze, 'I might as well drink it all away. I could drink a lifetime and not be rid of it'. Drunken rants because he was so unhappy, you know. Why? I don't even know. But nobody cared because we were busy ourselves, doing things that didn't matter. Spending money that didn't matter. Wasting time that mattered, but we didn't know it yet. Preoccupied. Self-absorbed. Blind."

She shook her head, looking pained. Eagan wanted to erase that expression from her face and never see it there again. But he knew the type she talked about. They came to the lodge all the time. Too much money and no sense of responsibility. They weren't villains, they were just too caught up in the abundance to focus on the things that really mattered. Like happiness and family and love for others.

"One night, he and my mama and my abuela went to dinner. They all had too much to drink, but papa drove home anyway."

Eagan's jag drew to attention, concerned because he could feel Clara's distress through their growing mating bond. He had a bad feeling he knew where this was going.

He pulled her to a stop, setting the tub aside, and turned her to face him. She stared at the ground as the rest of the story tumbled out.

"He blasted through an intersection, t-boning a car with an entire family inside. He was going twenty over the speed limit. The daughter was driving the other car. Just got her learner's permit. She... she was the only survivor between the two vehicles. She lost her mother, father, and tiny baby sister, all in a breath. In an instant, her entire family and half of mine was gone. Just... gone. And why? Because my father had a few too many and decided to drive?" She shook her head so hard her hair flew, and Eagan smelled the rank scent of tears.

"Clara..."

"No. See, it isn't that simple." She laid one

palm flat, facing the sky, and slapped her other hand on against it. "Basic. Break it down to basics. That family died because of *my* family. Me, my sister, my mama, even my grandparents, were too damn busy with our precious *things* to see how dangerous my papa was. We didn't care that he was ruining his life one bottle at a time. We didn't care until he ruined seven other lives. And we should have *cared*, you know? Who will care for you if not your family? Who?"

She stopped, breathing heavy with the weight of her confession.

"Then..." she gasped, and tears exploded from her.

Eagan drew her close, angry and wanting to fight away her demons, but unable to do anything but hold her. Shit.

"*Then* we cared," she sobbed. "After it was too late. *Then* things became simple. The way to prevent it clear, if only we could have seen it earlier. I went to see her one time, the daughter, to tell her sorry. Do you know what she said to me? She said, 'There is nothing to forgive. This wasn't your fault.' But she was wrong. It was my fault. If I had said, *papa, you don't need to drink*. If I'd said, *mama, don't let him drive*. If I'd done any of those things, I could have lived with myself in the aftermath." Clara cried into his shoulder. "But I didn't. I didn't do *anything* to prevent it. And the guilt... it was too much. It still is."

Eagan held her while she cried, while she let all the poison of her guilt out. His jag took it, held it, and when she was ready he'd help her let it go. She deserved to be free of her past, of her pain.

"I came to the woods because I needed things to be basic, simple. I needed to be alone and to think, and to realize how little I could survive on. How little I needed money. How very little I needed *period*. I didn't need a bed or TV or a bank account or... or... relationships. Life became easy and I could let go of the guilt. So much guilt. Even if just a little."

Pieces of his mate's puzzle began to click into place, and the picture it revealed gutted Eagan.

Maybe people wouldn't understand why Clara had chosen the woods, why she'd responded to her family's accident in this way, but he knew people grieved on their own terms. What was one person's way of working through tragedy, was another person's what-the-fuck. It was a lesson he'd learned from Magic. That cat had lost more than any of them, but if the same had happened to Eagan who knows how he'd have handled it.

"Aw, baby, this isn't on you. Or your family. Your daddy was a grown man who made lots of choices that brought him to that point in time, at that intersection."

She shook her head. "We could have made a difference."

"Maybe so. But..." Her way of thinking was inspiring. When he looked at it closely, it was so very much like an animal's. The basics. Instinct. Need. And purpose. "...but at base, isn't every person's choice ultimately their own? Doesn't each of us have to take responsibility for what mark we leave on the world?"

She pulled back, wiping her eyes, her brow furrowed. "That's true. But—"

"So, this is *his*. Not yours. This guilt over his choices, you need to let that go, Clara. You've learned from his mistake. You've grown and changed as a person. You don't owe the universe anymore."

Her mouth turned up, humorlessly. "Now I've got my own debt. Dug my own hole. I'm a *thief*," she sniffed.

A thief with a heart so big she'd mourned over burning ancient love letters. Letters that were boxed up and probably long forgotten, part of another lifetime altogether. So big, she took on everyone's guilt *and* her own.

Eagan kissed her forehead. "And you can dig yourself out. I have a plan."

She frowned. "What plan?"

"Your book. You want to make restitution for the things you've taken. Right?"

"More than anything," she breathed, and his heart melted at her vulnerability. "I want that so much, Eagan."

"Then that's what we'll do. If Magic will hear reason, we'll start working off your debt. Little by little, you'll pay back what you owe. And with each thing you mark off that list, the better you'll feel. Until your heart's as happy as it deserves to be."

Tears filled her eyes again, over-spilling her lids and sliding down her sweet round cheeks. "Why do you help me? Why are you so good to me?"

Eagan took her face in his hands, brushing her tears away with his thumbs. Slowly, he bent to kiss lips that were swollen from crying. Softly, he kissed her, relaying a message he wasn't ready to speak out loud. Again. And again, showing her that he thought she was precious, even if she was riddled with guilt. Both hers, and her family's.

He pulled back, staring into her eyes. "At base... you're mine. And I will *always* take care of what's mine."

His mate wrapped her arms around his waist, burrowing her head into his chest. And it was the best damn feeling he'd ever felt.

Mine, his cat purred. Always mine. My little woman.

THIRTEEN

"You've got to be fucking kidding me," Eagan bellowed, shaking his head. "Hell no. And again, *hell no.*"

Magic leaned forward, elbows on his heavy desk. "You want her to work off her debt, make amends? This is how it happens. The *only* way it happens."

"No. I won't do it. What you're asking is cruel."

"Cruel?" Magic spat. "What you pulled last night was cruel. Anchoring her to a futile mating is cruel. This? This is her salvation."

Eagan glared at the cat he once called brother.

"I'll hate you for doing this."

Magic narrowed his eyes. "I'll hate you if you don't."

"No." Eagan stood, sending his chair flying backward. "I won't do it. You find another way, or I'm gone."

Magic leaned back in his chair. "Go then. We don't need your kind around here."

"My *kind*?"

Eagan glanced at Renner and then Owyn.

"My kind." He let out an angry huff and threw his arm in the direction of the other cats. "Renner is my *kind*. Tana is my *kind*. Hell, maybe there are more of us who want to mate. The code has changed, Magic. The pact is obsolete. Do whatever you need to do to clarify that, but you can't ignore it. It's no longer 'No mating'. It's 'No straying'. A choice, not a result of our breeding. Get that through your thick-ass head."

Eagan shook out his shoulders, the disgust on his end this time. But what Magic was asking was out of the question.

"I won't take an oath to leave my mate unclaimed. I won't do it. Not even for the opportunity to work off her debt. Whether we mate will be *our* decision. Mine and hers. And most certainly not *yours*. Not some asshole faux-leader who let his mate die instead of promising her he'd stay faithful. That shit is yours, man. And you need to quit pouring it onto your clan. You need to own it, and deal with it."

Magic stood slowly, his whole body trembling with rage. "*Get. OUT.*" His roar blasted through the room like a siren of warning before a storm.

But Eagan wasn't done. And if Magic wanted a fight, he'd give it to him.

Owyn and Renner both stood from their chairs, shoulders tensed, clearly wanting in on the brawl. Well, fine.

"Shit," Owyn spat. "He's gonna change. Right here in the lodge. Motherfucking *shit*."

Eagan frowned, gauging Magic's behavior.

Oh. Owyn was right. *Shiiiit.*

"The back door," Owyn tossed out.

"No," Renner said. "It's broad daylight. Someone will see him."

Magic hated his cat more than anything. He fought the change, but it was gruesome to watch, his skin stretching and twisting as he struggled to remain human.

"Magic, man," Renner spoke carefully. "Just... calm down, yeah? Let's not make a scene for our guests."

But Magic's nostrils flared with his labored breaths. He might as well have been a bull fighting, for the sounds he was making.

Eagan shook his head, already defeated. There was no hope that he and Clara could live a life here with his family. None at all. Not if it reduced Magic to a raging monster.

With a burst of energy, the human gave way to the cat, Magic's panther unfurling from his skin in a furious flash of black fur.

"Fuck," Owyn barked when he got too close and the panther took a swipe at him. It was a warning, but still, those paws were the size of

Eagan's head, and the claws sharp as a sickle. They would have injured Owyn bad enough Doc Davis would've had to call for help.

"Son of a bitch," Renner muttered, starting to remove his clothes. He'd have to go full cat if he hoped to take Magic down like this. "Get out of here, Eagan. Take your mate and wait at the cabin."

Eagan stumbled for the door. There was nothing he could do here.

"And..." Renner glanced at him, frustration knitting his brow. "Have Layna tell the guests the noise is just us testing Halloween effects."

Eagan nodded and pushed through the door just as Magic's panther lunged at him, jaws snapping. He stared at the solid wood between him and the cat who used to be his friend, breathing heavy.

A hand touched his arm and he jumped.

Clara. It was Clara. She'd waited outside for him.

Gash came running down the hall, glaring at

Eagan and then snarling at Clara. He snapped his jaws and Eagan growled low in warning.

"What did you do?" the man spat, staring at Eagan like he was no better than a worm.

"Fuck you. Your turn's coming." The bastard watched Bailey too closely and it hadn't escaped Eagan's notice. The way his gaze gravitated to her wasn't casual.

Eagan grabbed his mate's hand and pulled her through the lobby, quickly relaying Renner's message to Layna.

She stared at Clara, a smirk on her face. "Don't worry, honey. The men around here are more hissy than the females, that's all. Things will settle."

Clara nodded, her eyes big.

"Let's go."

Eagan led her through the parking lot and back down the path to his cabin. Inside, he slammed the door, locking it, and leaning against it to catch his breath. He needed to shift just as much as Magic had. The energy balled up inside him like a grenade ready to blow.

Shift or fuck. Or both.

He looked at Clara. She stood in the middle of the room watching him.

"What happened?"

"He's an asshole."

"Magic?"

"Yes. He... he wanted me to promise never to mate you. If I agreed, he'd let you work. If I didn't... shit out of luck."

Clara looked confused. Of course she was. She didn't know their ways. He'd avoided telling her for too long.

"Eagan, explain this to me. About the mating. Everything."

He pushed off the door, stalking to her, and kissed her hard on the lips, pulling a gasp from her mouth. This was it. He was going to lay his cards on the table and hope she could handle it.

"We don't mate. Our clan, we don't mate. It's against the rules."

Her eyes went wide. "No sex?"

"Sex is fine. Mating is not."

"What's the difference?"

He reached a hand behind her head, pulling her hair free of its messy bun so it could tumble down her back.

"Mating is for life. A marriage of sorts. But one that bonds two people together forever."

Eagan watched her slender throat as it worked a swallow.

"Why is it not allowed?"

He kissed her again, sweet this time.

"Because cats aren't monogamous."

She went stiff in his arms. Suddenly he was holding a tree instead of a soft, luscious human.

"Excuse me?"

"Cat shifters as a rule, aren't monogamous. It goes against our animal's instincts. Our clan is the exception. We chose to abstain from mating instead. As young, we saw that it resulted in tragic pairings. Females so unhappy they don't want to live. Males so confused they can't tell instinct from reality. Families fractured and broken. Futures misshapen. We wanted better for ourselves. So we made a pact. No mating. Ever. Easy fucking peasy."

Clara squinted. "Your jaguar desires other women?" She laughed but it wasn't funny. "That sounds like an excuse to me. If you guys can't keep it in your pants, you just blame it on the cat? Do women really fall for that?"

If it was possible, Eagan fell even more in love with her in that moment.

"Yeah. Unfortunately, they do. But it's not a ploy. Not exactly. For males, our animals don't bond the way we want them to."

Clara frowned, shaking her head. "Poor Bethany."

Eagan didn't follow.

"I mean, it must be so hard to be mated to Renner and know he wants to be with other women." The look on her face was so sad.

"No, it isn't like that," Eagan huffed. "I'm trying to explain this, but I'm not doing it right. Too damn angry. Too..." He looked at her, standing there sad and confused. "Too needy. I fucking need you, Clara. But I have to settle first. So we can talk. You understand?"

"I'm trying to," she said, uncertain.

Eagan stepped back, pulling his shirt over his head. "I'm going to shift for a while. Okay? Pull my cat out. Just until I calm. I don't want you to be afraid."

"O-Okay. What should I do?"

Eagan thought about it. "Go lay on the bed."

Clara nodded and bent to take her boots off.

"Put on my clothes. The ones you slept in."

She bit her lip. "Are you sure that's a good idea?"

"Yes. Do it."

He unbuckled his jeans, removing the rest of his clothes so he was completely naked. Jag quarreled beneath the surface of his skin, needing something he couldn't give it. *Her.* He needed her, but she wasn't ready. Might never be.

He watched her as she stripped and dressed in the thread-bare clothes he'd loaned her and then laid on the bed. She stared at him expectantly.

"I won't hurt you," he reminded.

"I know." Her whisper of trust hit him right in the sternum, strengthening his bond for her.

Without any more hesitation, he let his cat roar forward, his flesh giving way to fur. His teeth to fangs. His hands to claws.

The jag purred with the transition and finally, finally being able to have his mate. He leaped forward, onto the bed, his massive paws on either side of her face. Her beautiful eyes were wide with surprise. And yes, fear.

Won't harm. Never harm mine.

Slowly, he lowered his nose to her neck, rubbing his face along her skin. A small giggle escaped her and it made him so happy he nearly forgot about the panther who'd taken a swipe at him.

"Your whiskers," she chirped. "They tickle."

His purr rumbled the room as he nuzzled her.

"Eagan," she breathed, and he felt the fear slip

away through their bond. "My Eagan. Can I pet you?"

Mate's hands. Yes.

His tongue darted out to lick her hand in encouragement. Leisurely, she ran her fingers through his thick black and tan fur.

"So soft," she murmured. "I never would've imagined."

He curled next to her on the bed, his paw resting on her shoulder while he licked her face. She giggled some more. He loved making her do that.

"You know," she said. "If you turn back into a man, we can talk this all out. And maybe... I don't know. Maybe you can lick me like that some more. Unless..." She laughed as his whiskers tickled her nose. "Unless I taste better as a cat or something."

Oh, his playful, naughty mate. How perfect was she?

He'd lick her alright. Lick her so good she'd think his tongue's only function was to give her pleasure. But first, he had some explaining to do.

***

Eagan's jaguar was a magnificent creature. He was huge with thick, muscular legs and paws the size of a dinner plate. She knew there were sharp, lethal claws in there somewhere but he was so very gentle with her, she couldn't be afraid.

He was completely Eagan. Kind and sensitive and concerned for her, even in his animal form. Why she thought he'd be any different, she didn't know. The cat and the human were the same. One man. Two forms.

It was amazing.

She leaned her head against him and stroked his fur, listening to the rumbling sound erupting from his throat. Gently, he nipped her shoulder and pulled back.

Between one blink and the next, he'd transformed. Taut, smooth skin replacing sleek fur. Cat eyes that almost glowed, replaced by the stormy ones she loved so much.

And he was naked. Lying next to her in the bed.

"Renner is completely faithful to Bethany. That's what I was trying to tell you. He's the only mated cat in our clan, and he's... different. He's decided to go a different route. A mutual mating, he calls it."

"A mutual mating?"

Eagan nodded. "See, the way it usually goes, the male finds his mate, claims her—whether she agrees to the matter or not—gets her with young, and then moves on to his next female."

"That's..." God, that was nothing Clara wanted any part of. "...*awful.*"

He reached across the bed to touch her cheek. "I know. But he always comes back to his mate. She's the one that matters to him. The one he protects at all cost. Monogamous or not, instinct demands we provide and care for our females and young. It sounds wrong, but male cats actually care deeply for their mates. There's a bond, it's just... flawed. And like I said, it lasts for life."

Clara frowned. "That doesn't make it okay to be with others."

"No."

"But your clan doesn't do this."

Eagan shook his head.

"And that's why Magic was mad when he caught us in the kitchen."

"Yes. He's uncomfortable because more and more of us are wanting to mate. He doesn't believe it's possible for us to deny our instincts to stray. But some of us want to be faithful. To raise a family with a female and be happy."

Clara considered it, her heart lodged in her throat. She'd never imagined herself in a long term relationship of any kind. But so much had changed in the last week. And Eagan made her want to try. But if he couldn't promise she was it for him... no amount of base logic was going to make her stay.

It left her feeling cold inside.

He was hers.

"What if Magic is right?" she asked quietly.

"He's not. Taking other lovers has nothing to do with our instincts. I know because of the way I feel about you. I want you happy and whole more than I want anything else. Me being with another female would never make you happy, so I have no desire to do it. That's my instinct. Being faithful is a matter of choice. And I—just like Renner— would choose to be faithful to my mate."

"To me."

He nodded solemnly. "To you, little woman."

The way he stared directly into her eyes, the way he spoke like this was the most serious topic in the universe... he'd thought about this. A lot. It wasn't some half-assed promise to get her in bed. He really wanted this, a mating with her. One that lasted for all their lives.

"So... a mutual mating."

"Yes. One where both make a commitment. Both are bonded."

"Bonded?"

He brushed her lips with his middle finger. "Yes, mate." His voice was dark. A summer's night like so many she'd spent outdoors. Sultry. "Ours has already begun. Every touch, every kiss, every shared moment, we draw closer to one another. Can you feel it? Our mating bond is already very strong."

"Yes." She could barely get the word out, because she felt exactly what he was talking about. She'd felt it earlier, when she spilled all her secrets to him. There was no one else in existence that she felt safer with, closer to.

It was only Eagan.

She sighed, running a finger down his bare chest. "I have so much to learn."

Slowly, a smile formed on his lips. He had the best lips. She could stare at them all day.

"Don't worry, Clara. I'll teach you." He rose up to tower above her, his hands braced on the mattress on either side of her head. Just like he'd done when he was a cat. "We should start with something functional, don't you think?"

His words shot right between her legs, and she bit her lip to keep from moaning at the idea of what he suggested. He was already naked. It would be so easy for them to come together. And it would mean something with him, she knew.

"Less functional maybe."

Eagan's gaze went instantly hungry and it lit her up even more. His eyes traveled downward to the peaked nipples that jutted from the t-shirt she wore.

"More sexual," he husked, tracing his finger around her beaded tip.

"Very sexual," she breathed.

He lifted his gaze, brow knitted, eyes burning hot with lust. Did he see that in her gaze too. Because damn it, that's how she felt. Lusty and hot and wild. She wanted to climb him like a tree and ride him like a bike.

"Sure you're ready?" His tone was hard, but she knew it was just because he was holding back.

She couldn't catch her breath for how powerful he was, poised above her, ready to do the most basic of bodily functions with her. He was pure, raw instinct and she knew it, needing her body to slake his. But she needed his too.

It didn't get any more basic than that.

She reached forward, wrapping her hand around his neck and yanking him down for her lips. She kissed him hard and urgent, like he'd done in the kitchen. She had to relay her message the old fashioned way because she was shaking with anticipation too badly to talk.

Eagan straddled her hips, one knee on each side, and grabbed her face with both hands. She was powerless like this. He decided which way her head went. He decided how much she moved, how hard they kissed, everything.

He explored her mouth like uncharted territory, even though he'd been there before, angling her for more of his tongue.

He pulled back, not even an inch, breathing heavy. "Your mouth, mate… it's so fucking sweet. I want to ruin it with mine. I want to kiss you so much, so often, that you taste like me. I want… I want… fuck, I want to make you mine, Clara. Mark you so everyone knows."

Yes. Do it. She was already his in her heart. Maybe she had been from the moment he'd cast judgment aside and shown her kindness.

But she couldn't get any of that past her throat before he kissed her again.

"Did you know," he said between nibbles to her jaw, "that I can smell you? Your arousal, it's filling up this cabin. Just how it should be."

"You can?" she squeaked.

"Mm hm." His heavy hand cupped one breast and her back arched into his touch. "It's making my jag crazy, baby. So fucking wild."

His attention was solely on her breast. That single one he couldn't quit touching. She squirmed beneath him, and in response, he closed his lips over the tightened bud, shirt and all. It was the single hottest thing she'd experienced to date.

But why did she have a feeling he was about to blow that right out of the water?

FOURTEEN

"Eagan, *please*," Clara moaned as her body shook beneath him.

Damn, her desire was beautiful.

Eagan lifted his head to watch her. "What is it, baby?"

She met his gaze looking bereft. Her mouth was open and panting. She was ready to come and her clothes weren't even off yet. He hadn't even touched her below.

His mate responded so perfectly to his efforts. It made him want to be perfect for her too.

He reached between her legs, cupping her

sex. "This?"

She clamped her thighs around his hand, and he was forced to move his hips. It was either that or explode, because his cock needed relief. He grinded it once against her hip.

"This functional thing?" he whispered, pressing the heel of his hand at the top causing her to let out a yelp. "Want me to show you what I can do to it?"

She nodded, tossing her head against his pillow. "Yes. God, yes."

Eagan grinned to himself as he eased down her body. Reaching behind her ass, he pulled the sweatpants down until they were bunched around her knees.

But then he stopped.

"You cut it," he croaked, when he got a look at the place he'd been waiting to own since she stripped to nothing right in front of him.

Clara froze, her eyes going wide.

"Your hair. You cut it." He stared at her, brow furrowed.

Her mouth fell open but nothing came out.

"Why?"

"I... I... it was getting wild. It needed its own zip code!"

He worked his frustration out with his jaw. "I *liked* it."

"You *did*?"

He nodded.

"Okay, well... I..."

"Don't do it again."

She bit her bottom lip hard with her teeth. "Yes, sir," she whispered.

He looked down at his mate's pussy. It was still wild. She hadn't managed to take it all off. He licked his lips.

"You look very pouty right now," Clara murmured.

Eagan shook his head. He felt pouty. "Don't do it again. Hear me?" He squeezed her thigh gently, softening his words. "Do not cut what's mine, little woman."

"I won't." Her voice was quiet, and he stared

up at her.

"Mine," he said softly, running the knuckle of his finger just barely between her folds.

She gasped, her stomach muscles contracting with each labored breath.

"Just so we're clear."

"Crystal clear," she confirmed, breathless.

Satisfied, Eagan slid his palm across the inside of her smooth, dark thighs, spreading her as far as the pants would allow. But it wasn't enough. He wanted her completely open to him. He wanted to see everything. Touch everything.

He jerked the pants further down. They caught on her ankles, and when he lowered himself between her knees, the material tightened, limiting her mobility.

Eagan met her eager eyes, smirking as he lowered his mouth to her slick flesh. Her scent was everywhere. He breathed deep, taking it in his body. Everywhere. Wanted that sweet scent all over him. He blew gently on her swollen lips and she jerked.

So sensitive.

"Did you touch yourself?" he rumbled. "In the woods, when you were alone, did you touch yourself?"

"Yes," she moaned.

"Good girl."

With a long, deliberate stroke of his tongue, he finally tasted her.

Eagan pulled back, staring at her wet slit, shaking all to hell. "*Fuck*." The words were barely a breath from his arousal moistened lips.

Clara stiffened. "What? What is it?"

She tried to sit up on her elbows, but his hand on her belly stopped her.

"Stay down."

"Eagan, what's wrong?"

"Wait. I have to make sure."

He bent to lick his mate again, his tongue delving into her over and over until she was limp beneath him once more. He could go crazy on her taste. Especially… especially this one.

He pulled back, his whole body trembling

with need, with what he wanted to do to her.

"You're in heat," he croaked.

"What?"

"You're fertile. Ready for me to put a baby in you."

"Holy shit," she cried, trying to lean up again.

"I won't," he said, nuzzling her short hair. "Not until your heart is as ready as your body. Now lay back. I wasn't done licking."

"But Eagan—"

He cut her off by pushing his tongue into her, slowly fucking her with it until she was too breathless to argue. Leisurely, he worked her, swirling his mouth over her clit and back to her opening. Her thighs quivered against his face and he knew she was close again. More urgently now, he sucked at her plump lips, nipping and lapping. Then he captured that swollen pearl at the top and she let out a cry so satisfying he almost released right onto the bed.

Fuuuuck.

She bucked against his mouth, and he

couldn't seem to stop giving her more. Even when she stilled, panting to catch her breath.

"Eagan... Eagan, please..."

He surged up, capturing her mouth, kissing her as she fell back to earth. "Please what?"

She shook her head, her eyes glassy with pleasure. "Just... please."

His gaze combed her body. She still had her shirt on. Damn shame. And he was torn, because the fastest way to have it off her was to rip it. But then, he *really* liked this shirt. Really, *really* liked it on her tits.

He shoved it up to expose those sweet peaks.

"Fuck me," he breathed. They were even better than he remembered. "Those are the best looking food bags I've ever seen, mate."

A second ticked by, and she busted out a laugh so hard it surprised him. His smile grew as he watched her tits bounce with her laughter.

"Yep. Totally functional."

She laughed some more and he sucked a hard nipple between his lips. But to his surprise, she pushed him back. All the way, until he was lying flat. She kicked the sweatpants from around her ankles and straddled his waist before he could think to stop her.

"I want more," she moaned. "All of you. Like you said. I want to make you mine."

Eagan's chest tightened with her words and his cock, which lay on his belly as she gently slid her wet pussy over it, grew harder.

He palmed her breast, sweating with the effort of doing the right thing. His cat was eager to fill her up. To mark her. But when he did that, it *would* be forever. His little thief would be his for life.

"We can't yet," he ground out.

Her plump lips worked him even though he wasn't inside her. His fingers dug into her perfect round ass, trying to stop her movement. Fuck, his woman was wild.

"Fertile," he managed, but she didn't quit sliding on him.

"I want it." Her moan filled the room and

made his cat purr.

Eagan leaned up to tongue her nipple again. "A baby? You want a baby?"

Finally, she slowed, and her hesitation made his stomach drop. But of course she wasn't ready for that.

Her small hands cradled his cheeks. "I'm your mate, right? This is part of the deal."

He shook his head. "Not yet. Not with everything in the wind. Not until you're ready."

Her eyes filled with tears. "I want to give you something. You've lost so much for me. It isn't fair."

"Baby." Eagan frowned. "I'm not an entry in your book. You haven't taken anything from me."

She chewed her lip, tilting her head to the side. "At base... I was made for you. My body, my mind..."

"Your heart," he added, making an X over the spot on her chest.

"My heart. I feel like this is right. Let me decide. You said I had to choose if I wanted forever. That this had to be mutual to work. Giving myself to you completely… it just feels right. Fertile or not." She lowered her eyes. "Unless…"

Eagan swallowed the ever-growing lump in his throat. "Unless what?"

She pressed her forehead to his. "Unless you aren't sure about us. About whether you can be… you know… faithful."

His hand on her jaw, he forced her to look at him. "I have zero doubts about that. Fucking none, do you understand me?"

"Then I'm ready," she whispered. "I'm ready to leave the woods and fix my mistakes and make a new life with you, the kindest, most caring man I know."

Her words left him breathless. Left his jag roaring.

"You're so fucking beautiful, Clara. Everything about you. I'm going to mark you. On your shoulder, right here." He brushed his fingertips lightly over her left shoulder blade. "With my claws," he murmured against her skin.

She trembled. "Y-you first though," she said, pushing him back down.

Eagan frowned, but let her. She swiveled her hips once more, wringing pleasure from him. Then she fisted his length, positioning it against her entrance.

"Baby, wait." He hadn't prepared her. She'd be tight after so long, and he was too big.

She shook her head, hissing as she pushed down and he breeched the first inch of her. Eagan drew in a sharp breath, determined not to slam home. She was blistering hot on him. Perfect. But he couldn't hurt her.

Patient, slow, his jag hissed. Never harm mine.

Never, Eagan agreed.

Clara took a deep breath, and with no warning at all, brought her hips down sharply, taking him in all the way.

Eagan choked on a gasp, fear slamming him in the chest. "Shit, baby," he croaked, sitting up to see her face. Her eyes were squeezed shut and she let out a whimper.

No. She was hurt.

He started to withdraw but her eyes flew open and she groaned. "Wait!"

He cradled her face. "Let me pull out of you so I can see how bad it is."

A drowsy smile curved her lips. "Bad? It's not bad. I needed you inside me. Now you're there. Don't go."

The muscles of her pussy contracted around him and his head fell back in ecstasy. She moved painfully slow, riding him like every tiny movement was more pleasure than she could take. This was like nothing else. He'd never made love like this, crazed one minute, heart-wrenching the next. His mind was utterly blown.

His wild little female. What was she doing to him?

And would he survive it?

***

Clara was all feeling. No thinking. The thinking was over. She'd made her decision and nothing she'd ever done had felt righter.

Right now, there was just this connection with her cat and the strangling mix of feelings it brought.

The bond. This was the bond Eagan talked about.

And it. Was. Everything.

His hands on her breasts, squeezing and caressing urged her on, and she rode him faster.

Staring down at him, she saw his eyes change, lit up in an unearthly way.

His jaguar.

On her next push, he thrust upward to meet her, his desperate fingers digging into the flesh of her hips.

Suddenly, her world flipped upside down and she found herself pinned beneath Eagan's powerful body. He dove for her mouth, lips moving passionately against her.

"I'm going to fill you up, and when I do, it will imprint you with my scent. Any shifter you meet will know you're mine."

His. God yes, to be his.

But...

"How will they know you're mine?"

Eagan slowed his thrusting to stare into her eyes. Dark brows slashed as he said, "They will see it in the way I look at you. The way I can't keep my hands off you. They'll know because I'm about to do something only one other cat has done."

"What's that?"

He drew back and pushed in once more, as if to remind her he was there.

"Happily—and I mean, ecstatically—forsake all others for my female. That's your mark, Clara," he said, dropping his face to nuzzle her neck. "You're branded on my heart, never to fade."

"Perfect," she murmured, determined not to cry at his beautiful words. Later she'd write them down in her journal so she'd never forget.

He moved again, grinding against her body until they were both breathless and strung to the point of breaking.

"Come on me, mate," he grunted. "Let me feel

you."

It was all the encouragement she needed as she shattered to pieces under him.

"Fuuuuck." His roar split the room.

Eagan tucked his hand under her shoulder, holding her in place for his final thrusts. His hard length twitched as he filled her, and she went numb from the pleasure.

A sharp pain at her back had her crying out, but he kissed it away as he continued grinding against her sensitive flesh.

His claws. The mark.

Happiness filled her until it leaked from her eyes as tears.

"My Clara," Eagan murmured against her breast. "My little woman. My sweet, sweet mate."

"My cat-man," she breathed, wrapping her arms around his head and hugging it tight.

Eventually their breathing settled, and Eagan slid carefully from her body. He rolled to the side, pulling her against his solid chest.

So right. So good.

"We..." He took several deep breaths before finishing. "We are functional *as fuck*."

Clara laughed, and he gingerly kissed the mark on her shoulder.

"We are," she agreed.

FIFTEEN

Eagan loaded the five gallon jugs of his famous hot chocolate onto the truck. Five of them ought to do it for the night. Next in was the giant trays filled with caramel apples and the bags of marshmallows.

It was Halloween. Three weeks had passed since Magic laid down his ultimatum. Three weeks since Eagan gave that thing the middle finger and claimed Clara.

Some of the cats were wary of his mating, he knew. But most had welcomed Clara into their clan with open arms when he'd made his intentions clear.

Eagan pulled the door closed on the truck and gave Bailey a wave. "Ready to go," he yelled.

She shot him a salute, and pulled out of the loading zone, heading toward the dirt road into the woods. The bonfire tonight would be the biggest and best of the season. All of his clan would be there and locals from Weston.

Except maybe not Magic.

He'd stayed clear of the big guy. It was the stipulation for them staying. Clara could work with Renner's crew preparing the haunted forest props as long as they both avoided Magic. Eagan felt bad about calling him out on his shit, if he was honest. But it was necessary. He had to get him thinking of the future. Thinking of his clan, and not crippled by fear. He wanted his leader to be happy. Maybe that disaster in his office was the seed that would grow the happy tree. A little pain before the gain.

He could hope.

He'd give Magic time to see the truth of

mating. That it didn't have to be a death wish for the females. That it was possible to love a single person so much, you wanted to rewrite history. Generations of it.

"Boo!"

Eagan jerked his head around to see his spunky little mate dressed in white flowing fabric. Her entire face and her long, curly hair had been painted white except for dark black circles that ringed her eyes.

A bit out of place, was her blazing smile. He'd never get tired of seeing that.

"I'm the Woman of the Woods!" She held her hands up, fingers wiggling in a mock-eerie gesture. "A ghost," she clarified.

Eagan grinned and pulled her close. "Oh no. I'm doomed. I've heard she steals souls and eats them for breakfast."

Clara giggled, shaking her head. "No, silly cat-man. She steals *hearts*. Not *souls*. And she eats cinnamon rolls for breakfast. In bed. After mind-blowing sex."

Her words grabbed him by the balls.

He lowered his mouth to her ear to whispered. "Mind-blowing, huh? Not functional?"

She smacked his chest. "I think we're waaaay past functional."

He nipped the shell of her ear. "I can't wait to get you home tonight."

Her aroused scent bloomed with his words and he did a quick look around to make sure no other shifters were near enough to scent it.

"Have you checked me today?" she asked, quietly.

Eagan pressed his nose to her neck and inhaled. There was no hint of a pregnancy.

"Not yet, little woman."

She frowned.

"But don't worry. I'll keep you to myself for a while longer." He grinned, reaching behind to pinch her ass.

Clara yelped and swatted his hand away.

"You aren't worried that it didn't happen?" she asked, unsure.

Eagan shook his head. "No. I'm happy. You're happy. I'm not worried."

She looked unsure. "Okay."

He forced her eyes to his. "You *are* happy aren't you?"

She'd worked hard with Renner's crew, and earned enough money to pay back everything she owed to the lodge and more than half of the items in her notebook. Just as he'd expected, with every item she replaced, her heart got a little lighter. She'd even made contact with her sister in Florida, and they were working through their past family hurts. Things seemed to be going according to plan.

"Of course I am. It's just... are you? Do I make you happy? Even with all the problems I've caused?"

"Do you make me..." Eagan laughed. This woman. None of her problems were really problems for him. Not when she was his to take care of. Not when she was his to love and have for the rest of forever. They were just details to be figured out. And he was good at that shit. "Do you see this goofy-ass grin? Do you think I'd wear this if I wasn't happy as fuck?"

Her lips crept up in her own grin. "It does look pretty dumb. You should probably stop it right away."

"Never," he said, kissing her white painted lips to seal his promise.

He pulled back and she wiped the makeup from his mouth.

"Let's go, mate. Sun will be down soon. We're going to be late for the scare fest."

Eagan looped his arm around her shoulders and led his female into the dimming woods.

Clara stopped suddenly, peering at a rock in the path. She bent low, squinting her eyes. Then they went wide with surprise and she made a clicking sound with her tongue. The tiny black head of a lizard poked out from under the rock.

"Hey there," Clara cooed, her voice going all soft with happiness.

The   thing   scampered   over   to   her outstretched hand and crawled up the sleeve of her gown.

"What's that?"

"My skink." She grinned wide.

"Your what?"

"My skink. He's a five-lined skink."

"Yeah. I know, but..."

She watched as the lizard settled on her shoulder. "He was my companion sometimes, in the woods. I thought he'd be hibernating by now."

Eagan glared at the thing. Before he could stop himself, he let out a loud hiss and the reptile slinked back into her hair.

Clara's eyes went wide. "Why'd you do that?"

"He smirked at me. I was telling him you're mine."

She laughed, standing on her tip-toes to kiss his cheek while the skink looked on from her shoulder. "It's true. You've got something the skink could never offer. It's kind of a deal breaker."

"Oh yeah?" He pulled her hips into his, letting

her feel his hardness. A reminder of what she'd get tonight after all the spooky stuff was over.

She nodded, a playful gleam in her eye.

"The skink can't cook."

****

Read on for a sneak peak of

Magic's story in book #2,

Ouachita Mated…

ONE

Magic stood on the footbridge that crossed a small finger of the lake that cradled the lodge. This was his. This lodge and the people in it. Even the visitors were his for a time. But the shifters and humans, the people who made up his clan, they were his responsibility. It was his job to keep them safe.

Even from themselves. But especially from each other.

He stared down at Renner's mate, Bethany, as she sat on a bench along the bank staring into the water. The bubble of sadness surrounding her disturbed him. Almost four years had passed since he'd allowed Renner to take a mate, and it wasn't a mistake he'd make again.

He hadn't decided what to do about Eagan and his human yet, but there was no doubt in his mind, allowing any of the cats to mate was a huge misstep.

Until a few months ago, Bethany had been happy. Magic had watched her closely over the years, gauging her for any signs of trouble between her and Renner. He'd promised Magic he was different, that he felt so strongly about Bethany his cat would never stray.

But Magic knew better. He knew it'd only take time before Renner's cat would bend to its instinct to bed another. Maybe he hadn't actually done it yet, but clearly, Bethany was feeling the heat and it made Magic want to smash someone's face.

Pulling his gaze away from the female, he stalked to the front of the lodge. Halloween cleanup was in full swing. There was much to do before Thanksgiving, and even more to pull off before Christmas.

Thinking of Thanksgiving left him mulling over his problem with Eagan. As head chef for the lodge, Turkey Day was Eagan's gig. It was his job to make their visitors feel as if they were enjoying the holiday from the comfort of their own home. Or even better, their grandma's. And he was good at it. Old Granny Whoever didn't have shit on Eagan's homemade rolls and cornbread dressing. And his gravy... he must put the dust of angel's wings in his gravy. There was no other excuse for it tasting so heavenly.

From a business standpoint, sending Eagan and his mate away would be crippling. But allowing them to stay could be damaging to his people. Already, he'd let Renner talk him in to letting them stay through Halloween. And people were taking to the wee little human with her unique ideals and her... lizard. The visitors thought the bastard thing was cute. They liked to pet it.

Magic shivered as he pushed through the front doors.

Layna rolled her eyes at him from behind the front desk of the lobby. "You're late."

"I'm the boss. There's no such thing."

She closed the ledger she was writing in and shoved it under the counter. "Funny. But I meant you're late for your appointment with Doc Davis."

Shit.

He glanced at his phone. He'd stayed on the bridge watching Bethany too long.

"She waiting?"

Layna nodded, smirking. For some reason she seemed to like seeing him screw up. If he didn't know she loved him like a brother, he'd think she hated him. He narrowed his eyes to a glare as he pushed past her.

Doc Davis was a werecat like the rest of them, except she had a PhD. Her office was just past the spa, and was where she treated anyone who needed help. Shifter or human.

Well, Magic needed help. He was man enough

to admit it. To himself at least. And Doc. To anyone else, he was fine. Middle-fucking-finger fine.

He knocked on the door and waited for her to ask him inside before edging it open.

Doc sat behind a heavy solid wood desk. Rows of bookshelves lined the wall behind her and a small leather couch sat off to the side. A second door led to an exam room full of equipment.

The female looked up from her work, peering at him over her thin-framed glasses. She was younger than Magic by a couple years, but had always seemed older. Maybe it was the way she pulled her hair back in the slickest bun imaginable, or that her glasses always sat too low on her nose.

She smiled. "Magic. What can I do for you today?"

He stared at the small sign that sat on her desk while he tried to think. *Christina Davis, M.D.*

"We had an appointment. What I talked to you about the other day. Remember?"

She sat back in her chair looking uncomfortable. "You realize I'm the wrong kind of doctor for this, right? I'm a medical doctor. Not a therapist."

Magic shrugged, his irritation growing. "A doctor is a doctor is a doctor. You're bound by patient confidentiality, right?"

Doc Davis frowned. "Yes, of course. But—"

"Then you're the one for the job."

"What is the job exactly? What do you want to accomplish with these... meetings?"

Magic thought about it. "I want to be able to say her name without losing my shit."

Even revealing just that much left him shaking like a newborn bird. He shoved his hands in his pockets so Doc wouldn't see.

Maybe he couldn't do this. Maybe it was asking too much of his panther to finally deal with memories of his mate.

But he'd lose everything he'd worked for if he couldn't learn to control himself. The fight with Eagan proved that. The mere mention of what had happened to Mandi, and Magic's cat had come out in the lodge, putting their guests in danger, and it was unacceptable. Luckily, he'd been contained to his office by Renner and Owyn, but it could never happen again.

Which meant Magic had to learn how to talk and think about Mandi without going all batshit.

He clenched his jaw so tight, he felt it pop.

Hells bells, he didn't think it was possible. Simply *thinking* about it was making him raw.

Doc pursed her lips, cocking her head to the side and looking him over. Like he was a puzzle she couldn't figure out.

And she was the one with the higher education.

"I don't know if I can help you, Magic, but you know I'll try my best."

He lowered his gaze to the floor. He didn't like appearing weak. And the way he was trembling, screamed weak *as fuck*. But Doc knew everyone's weaknesses, and never looked down on any of them. She was a damn good female.

"Why don't you sit down."

Magic cleared his throat, stiffly moving to the couch. He felt like a human accordion, folding himself onto the small furniture. Kicking one foot out, he tried to get comfortable.

"Where should we start?" Doc mused, tapping her finger against her chin. "Have you ever talked about that day? The day you lost her?"

He shook his head. "I can't go there yet."

"We all know what happened. People talk," she said carefully. "But I think you already know that."

Magic nodded, rubbing his palms together. It bothered him that people discussed his past, but it didn't surprise him. And they deserved to know about the person they trusted as leader.

"I'm not ready to talk about that night," he said again.

He looked around the office. It could be any doctor's office except for the collection of candles that lined one window and the multi-colored afghans folded neatly on the arm of the couch.

Those two things coupled with the wood plank walls made it feel a tad more homey.

"Then maybe you'd like to talk about how you feel."

Magic raised one eyebrow skeptically.

"What? Isn't that what therapists say? Look, I'm winging it here."

He shook his head, staring out the small window by the side of the couch. "Maybe I just need to start a diary or some shit."

"Is that what you need? Someone to listen to whatever you say and not respond?" She kicked her feet up on the desk. She wore hiking boots instead of those thick-soled things you saw in most hospitals. "I can do that. No problemo."

He stared at her. *Was* that what he needed?

"What do you think I need?"

One side of her mouth came up in a smirk. It would've lent itself more of a smartass effect if not for the way she peered over her glasses.

"Aw now, Magic. I could tell you what I think you need, but I doubt you'd want to hear it."

P. JAMESON

He frowned. "You're the doctor. Of course I want to hear it."

"Yeah, but this wouldn't be the doctor speaking. This would be Christina, your friend and clanmate."

Magic sat back and crossed his arms. He never liked knowing what his clan thought of him. He was a hardass, he knew. He made life difficult for their animals, he knew. But each of them had chosen to be here. They'd all agreed on the no mating pact, each for their own reasons. If any of them wanted out, all they had to do was say the word.

"Okay, Christina, my friend and clanmate. What do you think I need?"

She was doodling on a small notepad while she thought. He waited for what seemed like hours before she answered, but he knew it was only minutes. Maybe even seconds.

Doc held up the note pad to show him what she'd drawn.

"A heart? You think I need a heart?"

233

He wasn't heartless. He didn't like that his clan was incomplete without their mates. He felt their pain whether they realized it or not. It was just a matter of which pain was worse. Being responsible for the eroding of a female's soul, or being alone. Alone seemed better for everyone by far. But maybe they didn't see it that way because they hadn't lived it like he had.

"I have a heart," he said, disgusted by her answer.

She rolled her eyes over her glasses. "Obviously. Or you wouldn't be here right now. Love, Magic. You need love."

Don't miss the next installment in the Ouachita Mountain Shifters series, available now!

ABOUT THE AUTHOR

P. Jameson likes to spend her time daydreaming, and then rearranging those dreams into heartstring-pulling stories of trial and triumph. Paranormal is her jam, so you're sure to find said stories full of hot alpha males of the supernatural variety. She lives next door to the great Rocky Mountains with her husband and kids, who provide her with plenty of writing fodder.

For more information about P. Jameson and future stories, visit www.pjamesonbooks.com or find her on Facebook.

Made in the USA
Columbia, SC
19 February 2023

12532022R00145